WATERCOLOR
Whispers

Copyright ©2024 On Purpose Publishing LLC

Written by Suzette D. Harrison

All rights reserved. No part of this book may be reproduced or transmitted in any forms or means, electronic or mechanical, including photocopying, recording, or by any information storage and retrieval systems, without written permission from the publisher and author.

ISBN-13: 979-8-9886623-7-2

eBook ISBN: 979-8-9886623-8-9

This book is a work of fiction. Any reference to historical events, real people or real events is used fictitiously. Other names, characters, places, and events are products of the author's imagination and are not to be construed as real. Any resemblance to places, events, or real persons, living or dead, is purely coincidental.

Made in the United States of America

Cover Design: Jan Espanola, Ennel John Online Design

Project Editor: Nicole Falls, Trim & Polish Editing Services

Published by:

On Purpose Publishing LLC

P.O. Box 340012

Sacramento, CA 95834-0012

www.sdhbooks.com

Also by Suzette D. Harrison

Forever Beautiful
My Name is Ona Judge
The Dust Bowl Orphans
The Girl at the Back of the Bus
This Time Always
Basketball & Ballet
The Birthday Bid
The Art of Love
My Tired Telephone
My Joy
Taffy
When Perfect Ain't Possible
Living on the Edge of Respectability

Dedication

This book is dedicated to the artists, the creatives, the crafters &
makers who brush the world with beauty.
You are appreciated.
Thank you!

WATERCOLOR
Whispers

SUZETTE D. HARRISON

One

Mother said I barely cried when she gave birth to me. I'd been quiet, reserved ever since. Quietness, shyness, were intrinsic to my nature; some days they were my defense–a shield to hide behind when life felt discolored. Intense. My being the youngest, with four highly vocal and opinionated older sisters who'd appointed themselves as secondary mothers I didn't necessarily need, merely solidified that disposition. I was twenty-seven and married, but that hadn't lessened their bossy tendencies. Being born to Jonah and Maple Robertson—a woman who could talk Jesus off the cross only if long enough to still her rarely resting lips before climbing up on the cross and finishing His business—certainly didn't help any. Father's speech was impaired, and he rarely spoke now due to the stroke he suffered three years ago. Prior to this impediment he was more verbose than Mother, which was truly saying something. These loquacious people I called family. In the reverberating shadows of their noise, I existed—accustomed to being talked over; to silently, quietly retreating.

Except for here.

Two days each week I was the adult in charge of a room filled with little people under the age of majority. Here, I was seen. And heard. Admired, even.

"Miz R.B., I'm finished!"

I put a finger to my lips, reminding Packer Sims IV, best known as Peanut, not to disturb classmates still working on their art projects. My last name was hyphenated, the maiden with the married. Mrs. Robertson-Brinks being a mouthful, I'd allowed my students to shorten it to Mrs. R.B. But being southern and North Carolina bred, that was invariably shortened to Miz.

I motioned Peanut to the front of the schoolroom where I taught art every Tuesday and Thursday. Tuesday mornings were spent with the kindergarteners while my afternoons were shared with Profit Coleman Elementary's combined class of first and second grades. Thursdays were the same with classes in the morning and afternoon, except those times belonged to third/fourth graders, and fifth/sixth grade students respectively in this four-room schoolhouse, which was an impressive upgrade from the one-room structure in which I'd been educated.

My preference would have been teaching five days a week, fully utilizing my talents and sharing my gifts. But something was better than nothing. Teaching art twice each week allowed a delightful reprieve from endless domestic duties. Plus, it provided steady employment that even Willard couldn't find distasteful. For this, I was grateful.

For someone so determined that we save enough to move out of my parents' place, he sure finds something lacking with every job option ever presented.

My husband of three years habitually objected to any job opportunity that ever happened to come my way, finding something unsavory in each. Secretary. Cook. Staff writer for *The Colemanville Chronicle*. Colemanville was only yea big, not a wide city where vast job opportunities may have existed for women. His objections made me wonder if he feared my independence. As the teacher of the fifth and sixth grade combined class, Willard couldn't possibly find fault with my being invited to teach art here at Profit Coleman Elementary without looking hypocritical and foolish. Every Tuesday and Thursday I nearly skipped to work, thanking God for a place and the space to be me.

"My goodness, Packer, this is fascinating." Golden, autumn light streamed gently through the classroom windows as if I might need extra assistance deciphering my student's artwork. And I did.

Purple, pudgy, bug-eyed creatures sat atop blue and green misshapen balls of varying sizes seemingly sprouting from what may have been a field of popcorn.

After mistaking Suda Mae Jackson's painting of her newborn sister for a loaf of bread with pink slippers, I'd learned to withhold any observations and let my little artists educate me. That mitigated my misinterpretations as well as prevented hurt feelings.

"Have a seat here in the Sharing Chair, Packer, and tell me about your masterpiece."

I waited as Floretta's soon-to-be "son-by-marriage" plopped onto the chair I'd positioned facing me, alongside my easel, for these wonderful, one-on-one, artist-to-artist moments. Floretta, known to most as Flo, was so like her dearly departed mother, Iva, that she lovingly dubbed Packer IV her soon-to-be-son-by-marriage. She didn't believe in stepmother, stepson designations.

Ilona, I don't need a step in front of my name and neither does Peanut when we'll be bonded by love and marriage.

I smiled at the seven-year-old son of Flo's fiancé, thinking he was blessed to gain a second mother in Floretta after his left town years ago and failed to reappear.

"These're pumpkins. You know...to celebrate next week's Harvest Festival."

I scooted closer to the sharing chair and considered Packer's blue and green spheres. "I see. Very imaginative use of color. And these?" I pointed to the plump, purple creatures perched atop Packer's pumpkins.

"Those're frogs."

"And they're purple because...?"

"They ate too much."

"Ah! Let me guess. This field of popcorn that the pumpkins are in is the cause of the frogs' overindulgence."

"What's that mean...old-and-dull-gents?"

I choked back a laugh and offered the correct pronunciation as well as an explanation that Little Packer effortlessly grasped.

"Yeah, well that's what my frogs did, Miz R.B. They ate like my pa says I do sometimes when Nana's cooking's extra tasty. They ate like they ain't got good sense. But that ain't popcorn." He smiled proudly. "That's grits. With extra butter like I like it."

Dear Lord, don't let me laugh in this child's face!

I pulled a gold star sticker from the pocket of my art smock and handed it to him. "This, young sir, is for your bold and unconventional use of color. Well done."

"Mz. R.B., you sure do use some fancy words. I don't know what all 'un-convict-shell-naw' means, but I'ma take the star and just say thanks."

With that, Packer Sims IV strutted back to his desk, head high, proud of himself.

Flo has some interesting parenting ahead.

I smiled, appreciating Flo and I having grown close since her mother's passing last June. I'd painted and gifted her a portrait of Iva that brought Flo to tears and she'd hung in her salon to keep her mother close. We were eight years apart, but that painting brought Flo and I together as friends.

Joshua and Caleb seem to be faring a bit better than before.

I watched Little Mister Packer take his side of the bench-seat shared with his best friend, Caleb—Iva's youngest and Flo's baby brother—a sweet soul whose artistic renderings were less abstract than that of his seatmate. In my opinion, Caleb had a talent that deserved more time and attention and produced art on par with their brother, Joshua, who was a few grades ahead.

When school resumed last month in September, Joshua's art seemed angry, brooding with its dark palettes and jagged edges. Caleb's had reflected sadness in the constant drawings of familial scenes with mothers missing. Art was therapeutic and I never censored what the boys produced. Yet, it was comforting to see a reemergence of light in recent renditions.

"Packer. Caleb. Quiet please. Others are still working."

"Yes, Mz. R.B," they responded in tandem, same as they did most things.

Their smiles were nearly cherubic enough to make me reconsider my stance on being fruitful and multiplying.

I loved children. I simply didn't want any. At least not now. Or in the immediate future.

Not until my art has the full opportunity to become whatever it's destined to be.

The need to paint beautiful things burned within me. I was preoccupied with capturing God's glory. The sky. The tilt of a flower. Copper Lake. Humanity. And I believed in my God-given gift, that there was a place for it and that I *would* experience all heaven intended for it. Art exhibitions. Tours. Classes. Selling originals and reproductions. Even collaborations. Large or small, I believed my work had the ability to succeed.

I hadn't gone to Fisk University and defied my parents by

secretly changing my major from English to art for nothing. They'd been furious when learning of my deceit, but by then I'd completed so much of the art program that forcing me to withdraw—or to resume my English studies—would have made little to no sense. It took years for them to forgive me, and most times I felt I married Willard because he was *their* choice, and to get back into their good graces.

Tell the truth and flip the devil. Those're facts. Not feelings.

Yes, perhaps I married Willard for those reasons. And because Gabe was missing.

I shivered before shaking off unneeded thoughts of a man I'd loved more than he'd loved me. Apparently.

The sound of the timer I kept in my satchel interrupted unnecessary thinking.

"Class, it's time to clean up and prepare to end our day."

"But I ain't near 'bout finished, Aunt Ilona."

"I'm not nearly finished, Callandra," I gently corrected my niece. "And how should you address me here at school?"

"Oops!" She giggled and covered her mouth. "I mean I'm not nearly finished, Mz. R.B."

There was a decided age gap between my sisters and me. The daughter of my third-oldest sister, Olivia, Callandra was her late-in-life baby—same as I was for my parents—and my favorite niece.

I smiled and gave her a conspiratorial wink. "Who else needs more time on today's masterpiece?"

Several hands shot into the air.

"Those who need more time will have ten minutes at the start of class on Thursday. Those who don't will sit with me and read a colorful story while waiting for our fellow artists to finish."

"Yes, ma'am," rang out as if my class were a well-rehearsed choir.

"Yes, Packer?"

He lowered his raised hand at my acknowledgment. "Can we read *Little Red Hen*?"

Caleb spoke before I could. "Why you always wanna read that book?"

"It's got hot baked bread in it."

Tippy, Flo's cousin, claimed Little Packer had tapeworms and dubbed him a nonstop eating machine. With the latter, I was inclined to agree.

"Let's wait until then to decide which book to read. We'll also finish our Harvest Festival decorations on Thursday." I had to wait for their cheers to subside before continuing.

Someone, some time in Colemanville's history, decided Halloween was a day for uncouth, door-to-door begging children, Satan, and his minions. Per his or her hyper-righteous decision, there would be no trick-or-treating in our fine town founded on Christian principles. Instead, every October thirty-first, we were to celebrate the Lord's bounty with a fall Harvest Festival on the grounds of–weather permitting–First Jubilee AME that was sanctified and free of candy-begging, demonic activity.

"Everyone please hang your art to dry and clean your places. We have only a few minutes until school ends for the day."

My sixteen first and second graders quickly complied, using clothespins to carefully clip their pages to the makeshift collage station I'd fashioned with an old clothesline lowered to an appropriate height. Once finished, they gathered about me where I sat behind my easel.

"I'm proud of everyone for having such a beautifully artistic day." I made eye contact with each student long enough to convey that I saw and honored them. "We have a lot to do on Thursday, so come with your art hats on and your artist fingers good and ready."

I stood and placed my hand on my chest, prompting them to do likewise as we cited our artistic allegiance.

"We are the wonderful colors of God's precious palette. We make the world a prettier place with our rainbow of radiance."

I followed with, hand yet on my chest, bowing to each student as they exited.

"Sorry for calling you Auntie Ilona, Mz. R.B." My youngest niece, Callandra, was the last to leave.

I hugged her fondly. "Thy sins are forgiven, Callie."

She giggled merrily. "Are y'all coming for Daddy's birthday dinner tonight?"

"We'll be there promptly at seven," a male voice announced.

We turned to find my husband in the doorway, satchel in hand, staring at the small splotch of paint marring my niece's dress, disapproval souring his expression.

"Hi, Uncle Willard." Callie waved cheerfully, unimpacted by my husband's disdain. "Mama's making extra fried chicken and greens 'cause she knows you don't like to do nothing but eat."

I busied myself packing my satchel, praying Willard had had a good day and wouldn't be bent out of shape by my niece's forthrightness.

I glanced at him, thinking Willard Brinks was nice looking, with his toasted almond-colored skin, fastidious grooming, and round spectacles that emphasized his studious nature. But his penchant for all things fried or sweet had resulted in an unhealthy amount of extra girth on his five-foot-eight-inch frame. He complained of joint pain, sweated easily and profusely, and was too often out of breath.

None of that curtailed his overconsumption.

"Run along, Callandra. Your schoolmates are waiting." Willard's tone and expression were dismissive.

My niece kissed my cheek and skipped toward the door.

Willard scuttled backwards, creating distance between him and Callie as if the paint splotch on her dress might be contaminating.

For a teacher who claims to want children, he sure acts as if they're off-putting.

He addressed me from the doorway. "I trust you had a good day, but you shouldn't wear that dress. Either it shrunk or your hips are expanding again."

My weight hadn't changed since we met in college whereas Willard's pants size had increased four times in three years. Clearly Callie's comment *had* bothered him, and he was firing that irritation in my direction. Doing so was unwarranted, yet I said nothing while moving toward him.

"Let's get home." He labored down the short hallway. "I have assignments to grade before dinner. And being that it's Tuesday...we shan't dilly dally at your sister's."

Tuesdays. Thursdays.

I walked alongside my husband with those days etched in my brain as the only days Willard wanted and permitted marital relations.

Two

One would think we were experiencing an insufferably hot summer day versus the cool of autumn the way Willard carried on as we walked home from the schoolhouse, his disposition cranky.

I had to break up a dispute over marbles between a group of sixth graders during first recess.

Not one, but two *students failed to turn in their science projects.*

And those Claxton twins have yet to master good hygiene practices.

He whipped his handkerchief from his jacket pocket and mopped his forehead every few steps, recounting the woes of his workday with labored breaths.

I tried to be a suitable and supportive wife so tuning him out wasn't intentional. But Willard's dissatisfactions and souring disposition seemed to have increased since we'd married and multiplied exponentially daily. I was hard-pressed to keep up with them. I'd already offered dutiful reassurances that he was a wonderful educator respected by his students, but that didn't penetrate the vile mood he was in.

I gave up trying to be uplifting and resorted to punctuating his deluge of woes with noncommittal sounds that were little more than "mmm" or "uh-huh," and he failed to notice. He was caught up in Willard World and wouldn't reemerge until his woes were fully aired.

Clearly his woes were many. His morose monologue lasted so long that we were in the downtown district a few blocks from home when I dared to quietly ask a question that made him even more irritable.

"Willard, are you happy?"

That stopped him in his tracks. He stared at me as if I'd called his hero, Booker T. Washington, a one-eyed, three-legged, bucktoothed communist. "Of course, I'm happy! What an outlandish thing to ask."

He resumed walking, *and complaining*, unaware that I lagged behind without accompanying him.

It's a splendid day to appreciate Colemanville.

Of necessity I turned my thoughts elsewhere to avoid being infected by my husband's bellyaching. I paused on that downtown walkway to absorb the colors of our small town, thankful for its beautiful ability to offset Willard's peevishness.

Azure skies. Thick cotton candy clouds. Golden autumn light. A mahogany rainbow of humankind. And scents so heady they might as well have been colors from the jasmine and lavender fields nearby. I was already painting its glorious landscape in my mind's eye.

"Ilona! Little girl, when you making time to pretty up my storefront window?" Miz Grayson waved from across the street, gaining my attention.

That left me laughing at our small-town competitiveness.

Since painting *Iva's House of Beauty* in gold on the window of the salon a few months back, downtown merchants had been urging me for similar treatment. Signage painting wasn't beneath me, but I'd only done Flo's place because Iva had been such a gem, and to help lift Flo's spirit after her mother's passing. I had no desire to be the town signage painter, hopping from one business to the next—changing and repainting designs every time a proprietor was possessed by a new whim.

"My apologies, Miz Grayson. I'm busy at the schoolhouse working with the children, but I'll see what—"

"My wife'll gladly oblige you, ma'am."

I stared at Willard as he backtracked to where I stood, wondering when he'd become the god of my time and talents. Was this the same man who'd turned his nose up and accused me of demeaning myself when I'd painted the window of Flo's salon?

He lowered his voice when reaching me. "That penny pincher probably won't pay much, but we need the money. You know," he whispered. "A place of our own. A baby."

I inhaled deeply rather than remind him I wasn't ready for children and doubted we'd ever make any. Not with his scheduling marital relations twice a week as if business meetings.

Business meetings are probably more interesting.

I shied away from that thought, afraid I was taking on Willard's grouchy disposition, and promised Miz Grayson I'd be in touch when time permitted.

"Time permits. You only teach twice a week." Willard turned toward home with a new topic of grousing: me. "Besides, it's not really educating. Not like the core essential subjects I teach. Such as science and mathematics. Yours is more casual and social...you know...playing in paints with children. Painting storefront windows might be beneath a Fisk alumnus with an art degree. But it's more than what you're doing."

Being married to Willard Brinks these past three years had offered adequate time to grow numb to his insults. And to develop thick skin. Yet, I meant to interject, to quietly remind

Willard of my daily contributions. Cooking. Laundry. Cleaning. Helping Mother manage Father's invalidism. But I didn't come to my defense. I couldn't. Not when seeing Gabriel Thurman.

I should have been up ahead with my husband. Instead, my feet felt glued to the walkway as I watched Gabriel Thurman in action. Thankfully, he was too busy carrying what looked like a curio cabinet to a customer's car to notice me visually absorbing the beauty of his being.

Tall. Broad but in a muscular way. Chestnut skin smooth as a melted candy bar left in the windowsill on a blazing summer day. His eyes were the color of warm honey; his handsomeness was seemingly limitless. But it was his heart, not the flesh, of the man that I'd fallen in love with.

Gabriel "Gator" Thurman.

I felt foolish watching his every gesture, but my unmoving feet stranded me, had me admiring a man who'd fought in the war for this country and come home seemingly the same yet invariably changed. Less talkative. Distant. At least from my perspective. But then again, my first love and I hadn't shared the same air or encountered each other much since his return to Colemanville three months ago.

Iva left this earth in June. Gabe came home in July.

Four years *after* the war ended. In 1949!

Rumor had it he'd spent time up north and out west after the war ended and found his way home only after his oldest brother, Budd, suffered a heart attack. His reasons for staying gone so long weren't my business, but I was glad he was relatively well after sacrificing for a nation that failed to realize the worth of a Colored man.

"Thank you, Gator."

Clearly, based on her excessive skinning and grinning, Pamela Sue Minkins held him in high regard. According to my dearest friend, Greenie, Pamela Sue, best known as Pumpkin, was an eyelash-batting, man trap with a backside the size of a mattress.

I bit my lip to keep from laughing at the memory of Greenie's uncharitable description. I'd been too busy watching Gabriel to notice Pumpkin was his customer but now she had my attention.

She'd eased up on him so close her sizable bosom grazed his chest. "Can I offer you some dinner this evening, Gator?"

I'd never addressed Gabriel by that nickname during the course of our relationship. It seemed so reptilian. Nearly vicious. I preferred the birth name he shared with an archangel. It was fitting for a man so gentle, celestial.

"I appreciate the offer, however—"

"Ilona!"

Willard's bellow interrupted Gabriel's response. I watched Gabe search one direction, then the next until those honey-colored eyes settled on me. His expression housed surprise, and something not easily identified. It was tight. Smoky.

Whatever the sentiment, he harnessed it and returned his attention to his customer, ignoring me. "Enjoy the curio, Ms. Pumpkin. It was a pleasure making it."

"Honey, you're nothing but pleasure in the making."

A grunt was Gabe's only response.

I watched him mount the walkway and head toward his family's furniture store, his shoulders back, head held high without arrogance. More like hard-earned confidence.

His right side was toward me, granting me full view of the indisputable way in which the war had changed him.

Staring was impolite and I wanted to avert my gaze, but there was something arresting about the vacant space where his forearm had once been. Now, the sleeve was partially empty and pinned at the elbow, proof that he'd left part of himself on the battlefield.

"Ilona, we'll be late to dinner!"

As a newcomer who'd moved to Colemanville after we'd married, Willard wasn't privy to the past I shared with Gabriel. His impatience wasn't fueled by jealousy, but by the notion that I could cause a meal to be delayed.

I hurried forward, ignoring Pumpkin Minkins standing beside her car watching me like a hawk does its prey.

My brother-in-law's birthday dinner proved a festive family affair. My parents. Sisters and their spouses. Nephews and nieces. That made for a loud, boisterous mix. It was love-filled, fun-filled but I was exhausted by the time the food was put away, the birthday cake cut and served, and the kitchen was clean.

"Ilona, I put food aside for y'all. It should last the rest of the week."

I thanked my oldest sister, Theodora, pretending not to hear my sister, Viola, two years her junior, remark that it might not last three days with Willard. Her observations weren't hurtful as much as they were too accurate. After several minutes of hugs and farewells, I helped Willard get my father into the car, dreading what was ahead.

My parents' house, the home I'd grown up in, wasn't far from Theodora's. With Willard driving my father's 1939 Pontiac as if he had an important appointment, we were home in minutes. I helped Mother get Father cleaned and dressed for bed after storing the food my sister had sent in the Frigidaire.

The stroke my father suffered three years ago greatly distorted the left side of his face and impaired his speech. He held his left arm close to his body as if in a sling. He had use of both legs, but his right was weakened, and he'd recently become prone to falling. That, combined with his slower gait, had prompted Mother to acquire a wheelchair from Flo's father, Doc Everett.

I hadn't agreed with her decision.

Father was a proud man and, for him, his dependence on us was difficult enough. Confining him to a wheelchair when he still had the ability to walk could reduce his sense of autonomy. I expressed this to Mother, quietly and respectfully, but she brushed my concerns aside, saying she knew what was best for Jonah Robertson. Afterall, *she* was his wife.

A year had passed since acquiring Father's wheelchair. It seemed to further reduce him and his faculties to the point that sometimes the Jonah Robertson I'd grown up with seemed a figment of my imagination.

"Mother, do you need help with anything else before I turn in?"

"No, dear, and thank you. We're fine. Go ahead and tend to Willard. Good night."

I kissed her forehead and rounded their bed, offering Father a good night kiss as well.

I was caught off guard when he grasped my arm with his good hand as I turned to leave. My parents had me in their mid to late forties and were now in their early to mid-seventies, respectively. Age combined with my father's failing health left me struggling to understand his garbled speech.

I looked at my mother, needing her help as an interpreter. Not to understand what Father said, but why he said it. Mother was busy retrieving Father's medicine from her bedside stand and pouring a glass of water from the decanter kept there for such purposes.

"Here, Jonah, dear. Take your medicine."

Father released me, his arm flying upward with such unexpected intensity that Mother lurched backwards. Water sloshed from the glass, dousing the front of her nightgown.

"Goodness gracious, Jonah! You've got me all wet."

I rushed to the hallway and grabbed a towel from the linen closet. Mother was pulling a fresh nightgown from her chest of drawers when I returned. She took the towel, assuring me she and Father were fine and shooing me off as if I were a fly.

Softly, I closed their door behind me, telling myself I'd heard my father incorrectly.

Forgive me.

Jonah Robertson was of the old vanguard, a Colored man who'd looked the hardness of life in its face without backing down. He was the son of Cain, a man rescued from slavery who became one of the founders of Colemanville. Father was proud. Erect in character. Not overly given to sentimental displays. And I certainly couldn't recall his ever asking my forgiveness for anything.

At least not with unshed tears in his eyes reflecting tortured emotion.

I slowly headed for the room I shared with Willard, puzzled and wondering if such softness and repentance was attributable to his illness. Or was some unknown ghost in Father's past rising to haunt him?

Three

Henry Ossawa Tanner's The Banjo Lesson.
No. Norman Lewis's abstract expressionism.
Or...Horace Pippin's pyrography and oil paintings.
Wait! Augusta Savage's sculptures and Jacob Lawrence's incredible collection.

I lay on my back mentally visiting the magnificence of some of my favorite Negro artists as Willard struggled to breathe on top of me. His movements lacked rhythm and were mostly jerky. That wasn't out of the ordinary. Nor was the feeling that I was drowning in a sweaty, unpleasant sea. The fact that he wouldn't be much longer, that he usually finished rather quickly, provided a sense of relief as my thoughts skipped back to Horace Pippin.

Mr. Pippin's pyrography—his decorated art created with the controlled use of heated objects such as a poker or pen-like tool—was nothing short of brilliant.

And to think a war injury led him to it.

He was a military veteran, a soldier shot in World War I

defending a country that couldn't seem to like, let alone love, us. Mr. Pippin had taken up art to help alleviate the injury to his right shoulder, for its therapeutic benefits.

I wonder if Gabe's woodwork gives him therapeutic relief.

I bit my lower lip realizing how indecent it was of me entertaining thoughts of Gabriel Thurman while in my husband's company.

Thankfully, Willard didn't notice. He was preoccupied with conducting our twice-weekly business. Plus, the lights were off and darkness shielded me.

Ilona, you realize you've never seen Willard's...anything?

Only shadows and silhouettes.

Since the day we were joined in holy matrimony and consummated our marriage, Willard insisted the lights remain off during our time together. According to him, doing bedroom business in the dark was sacred. As were marital relations. He was a devout Presbyterian who found demonstrative worship distasteful. He brought that same sentiment into our marriage bed, and was opposed to "unnecessary fuss and ruckus."

Our connubial time was always orderly. Brief. With only the sounds of Willard's heavy breathing. Until he reached a dangerous point of excitement. That was when he withdrew and hurried to the bathroom to bring himself to completion while I was left alone in our dark room staring at the ceiling.

My husband never finished inside of me.

And he and everyone else dares to wonder why I struggle to get pregnant.

Not that I wanted to be. Not at that moment. That didn't mean I wasn't curious about how things might be between us if Willard allowed himself to release while with me. I wanted to experience, if not fuss and ruckus, *something* versus a constant nothing.

It was taking Willard longer than usual to finish and I chose to occupy my mind and time. All he needed was my body to be present. He wouldn't notice my mental or emotional absence.

Scuttling away from intimate disappointment, I resumed cataloging my favorite artists.

Aaron Douglas!

How in the world had I started my list of honored favorites without citing Aaron Douglas?

I didn't simply admire Mr. Douglas or his work from a distance. I'd been blessed to have taken classes with him while enrolled at Fisk. The same university that was the home of the famed Fisk Jubilee Singers had become a lecture hall and art salon to that Harlem Renaissance wonder. Mr. Douglas, his murals, and illustrations in magazines like the NAACP's *The Crisis* lured me away from majoring in English with the intent of becoming a teacher, to opening what my parents considered my Pandora's box—my love of art, which included photography. I wound up trading the study of grammar, syntax, and ancient white poets looking nothing like me for sitting in Mr. Douglas's lectures or putting brush to canvas in his art classes. He was passionate and purposeful, insistent that Negro art was a divine part of our culture. Our pursuit of art was as significant as another student obtaining a degree in law or medicine. We were the keepers of our culture through artistic expression.

Gabriel always said my paintings were breathed on by the ancestors.

I closed my eyes, once again mortified by my wayward thoughts. Perhaps they were the result of encountering the first and only man I'd ever loved downtown today. Of being close enough to see how neatly his empty sleeve was pinned. Or the haunting honey color of his eyes and the shape of his full lips.

Those lips. I've kissed them. Tasted them. I miss them.

I squeezed my eyes tightly, wanting Willard to hurry up so I could wash my face and perhaps take a cool bath. I was hot beneath his bulk. Or perhaps I was warm due to unsanctified thoughts. Of Gabriel's lips. His height. Those broad shoulders. His hands on my hips.

What are your hips doing?

I realized they were moving. Slightly, but definitely. Something they never did in bedroom transactions simply because my husband thought it indecent. Still, I let them.

I gave myself permission to feel what I felt, even if it was stimulated by thoughts of my first love.

"Ilona, enough!"

I froze at Willard's gruff command even as he continued thrusting, pushing until, for the second, perhaps third, time in our marriage, his motion caused me to nearly feel something. My heart pounded with premature anticipation only for my husband to withdraw so swiftly a pain shot through my lower region.

He was deaf to my sharp, painfilled gasp as he jumped from the bed, intent on the bathroom where he could privately finish what was, obviously per his thinking, far too sacred to share with me.

He didn't make it.

An odd, strangled sound erupted from his throat as he braced the wall with his free hand before collapsing against it.

"Are you okay, Willard?" I righted my nightgown and scooted toward the edge of the bed, ready to offer needed assistance.

He remained in the dark, leaned against the wall breathing heavily. "I'm...fine... Just give me a minute."

I sat, uncertain of what to say or do next.

"Actually...I feel unclean and need a bath."

I stood swiftly. "I'll run the water for you."

"No." He waved me back. "I'll handle it myself. You've done enough."

He slipped on his robe and left the room.

I returned to bed feeling scolded. And unnecessary. Clearly, my being present during his release had caused him embarrassment.

This makes no sense!

Neither did our relationship. We were married in the eyes of God *and* under the law. Yet Willard acted as though our intimacy was sinful. As if I contaminated him in some way. His habitual finishing alone in the bathroom felt like something out of the Bible. Like he was some overly sanctimonious Old Testament zealot afraid of spilling seed in the company of a harlot, as if I was unholy.

"Defraud ye not one the other, except it be with consent..."

The curlicues of our brass headboard felt cool through the cotton of my nightgown as I sat with my back pressed against it, softly quoting the fifth verse of First Corinthians chapter seven. It was sufficient indication that I wasn't the unholy one in violation of God's ordinances. The Bible ordained marriage. And I'd never defrauded or withheld myself from Willard. Neither had I imagined being married but, for all practical purposes, celibate.

Maybe celibacy wasn't the best way to describe what I had with Willard. Admittedly, I was unsure what it was and sometimes I wanted to confide in someone. My parents were nearly elderly and a sizable age gap existed between my sisters and me. They were a different generation raised in a different time period, with stricter norms and expectations. I was uncomfortable discussing such issues with any of them. So I tucked the matter away and kept things to myself.

If I'm not mistaken, didn't that same verse say something about not giving place to Satan?

My thoughts jumped from an inability to confide in my family to that Bible verse again. I reached over and turned on the lamp. My Bible on the bedside stand wasn't merely decoration. It was there to solace me during Willard's abandonment, his restroom escapes.

Opening it, I softly read aloud the conclusion of the scripture.

"...and come together again, that Satan tempt you not for your inconsistency."

I was perplexed, not tempted. Maybe something *was* wrong with me as Willard often intimated.

I glanced up as he reentered our bedroom before I could give the issue further consideration. "Did you enjoy your bath?"

He barely grunted and climbed into bed. "Please turn off that lamp. Some of us have work tomorrow and need our rest." He placed a stingy kiss on my cheek, burrowed beneath the covers, and within minutes was sound asleep. And snoring.

I wonder if things were this way between Conroy and Greenie?

My dearest friend since childhood shared two whole years of what seemed to be marital bliss and true contentment with Conroy Simpson before losing him to leukemia. She'd been so broken by the loss that it seemed she'd never recover. At least not sufficiently enough to enjoy whatever blessings life might still offer.

Five years had passed since then, and she was better, if not completely healed.

But then again, losing the love of one's life created holes in the soul that didn't necessarily close. You simply learned to live with them.

I did.

Pushing that thought away, I repositioned myself toward my husband. His back was to me, but I pictured his face and reminded myself I was blessed to have him. I touched his back lightly, wanting human contact even while telling myself the past was finished and didn't need to be revisited. Especially when it involved Gabriel Thurman.

Four

Autumn's golden light floated through the open window with ballerina-like grace. It caressed my canvas, kissed and warmed my face. Alone in the backyard tool shed I'd converted into a studio, she was a welcome visitor in my quiet solitude.

One Saturday, with Greenie's help, I'd painted the inside walls a soft cerulean blue like the sea and mounted shelves for my plethora of supplies. Brushes. Paints, acrylic and watercolors. Charcoal sticks. Colored pencils. Sketchbooks. Palettes. Canvases. And more. The tools of my passion surrounded me like sweetly kept secrets or attentive fairies in this, my safe place and sanctuary.

The tool shed was a decent size, but otherwise it wasn't much. At least not the exterior. I'd left that as it was and concentrated my energy on its interior. There was no electricity. Willard and my parents considered installing electrical lines in the shed a waste and a fire hazard. Lanterns and candles had to prove themselves sufficient. Plus, in their opinion, my duties as a married woman didn't allow for extracurricular activity when my husband was home from work. Therefore, illumination for artistry by night or in the dark was, according to them, never needed.

"Well, he's at work and I'm free."

The house was clean. Laundry had been folded and put away. There was no need to cook considering the food we'd brought home last night from my sister's. Father was napping. Mother was reading and prone to doze off mid-paragraph. That left me with a few hours before Willard's return from the schoolhouse and I wanted to make good use of them.

Except I couldn't.

I sat at my easel staring at the blank canvas in front of me as if it was responsible for creating whatever would be.

"My goodness, Ilona. What's got you all upside down today?"

I'd seemed rather off since feeling something with Willard last night that never culminated. Whatever I'd felt had been aborted so quickly that, lying in the dark night with my husband's snores surrounding me, I told myself it was simply my imagination.

You can buy that lie or admit your nasty woman thoughts of Gabe Thurman.

"Focus, Ilona."

I slammed the door on errant ideas and twirled a paintbrush between my fingers, frustrated by my lack of inspiration.

I relished any and every opportunity to be alone in my safe haven of a sanctuary. To paint. Sketch. Draw. Create. And unfurl myself in the welcoming arms of art. Time and opportunity had been slim lately thanks to assisting with preparation for the town's autumn festivities that were soon happening. Next week's annual Harvest Festival on October thirty-first. The apple-picking at Greenie's toward the middle of November that, weather permitting, included a picnic for those who participated. And a night of hot cider and pie in the town square to mark the first of December.

Having a free afternoon was a gift. And my muse was forfeiting it.

"I have no idea what to paint."

Paint anything. Even if it's purple frogs in a field of grits.

I laughed brightly, remembering Little Packer's masterpiece yesterday, but laughter dried up like water drops in the desert when thoughts of his father surfaced. Or better put, those thoughts included visions of Big Packer with his best friend.

Gabriel "Gator" Thurman.

I hopped off my seat and grabbed the wooden, hand-carved box I kept on a back shelf. It was square, its size suitable for a man's hat, and was a beautiful piece of workmanship created in my final year of high school that I still cherished.

"It really is an exquisite collaboration."

The outcome of a class assignment, the intricate carvings on the sides of the mahogany box were matched in beauty by the painting on its hinged lid of a glorious hummingbird in delicate flight. I loved hummingbirds and this rendition was a vibrant jewel of green and blue with fuchsia decorating its tail and wings. It glimmered as if actively in flight beneath its lacquer covering. Opening the box, I ignored the heart-encased initials carved inside the lid and searched its contents until I found an old, torn photograph. Two Colored young men grinned into the camera—arms about each other's shoulders—looking as if the world might bend for them. I flipped the photo over to read the date on the back, ten years ago, May 1939. Long before Packer met Rudie and had a son. Before Gabe went to war and sacrificed an arm.

I trailed a finger over the planes of his face with its beautiful bone structure. Even back then, his youthful frame housed shadows of strength. And magnificence.

I shimmied away from what could be misinterpreted as lust to focus on the photograph in its totality.

"It's one of my favorites."

It was the first photograph I'd ever taken, back when being a photographer was my dream and M'Dear, my beloved grandmother, had gifted me a camera for Christmas when I was sixteen. My parents were less than supportive and considered M'Dear's gift a wasteful indulgence that I fell in love with.

That camera went with me everywhere like an extra appendage. That was until Mother took it and locked it away, threatening to toss it in the fireplace if I didn't "get serious" about going to college and studying English.

In my parents' opinion, photography was a ludicrous hobby that made about as much sense as me preaching to pigs. It wasn't something I could parlay into a career. Nor did it offer racial uplift.

You'll attend Fisk and earn a degree, then come home to put it to good use.

Except Willard had included himself in a group of friends I'd invited home from college one Thanksgiving and somehow made an indelible impression on my parents. Seemed as if I'd barely completed commencement before they were trying to marry me off to him, a man who didn't believe in female independence, as if we lived in the Far East in ancient days and were subject to arranged marriages. I'd managed to hold everyone off for two years, capitulating only after it was clear Gabriel Thurman had no intention of returning to Colemanville. Or to me.

I closed my eyes against an unexpected wave of sadness before refocusing on the joyful beauty of the box I held.

"Thank you, Mr. Gordon Parks, for proving Colored folks can make a living with their art. Whatever form it takes."

Placing that cherished box on the small table I kept beside the easel, I held the photograph up as inspiration, feeling proud of Gordon Parks, a brilliant photographer born in 1912 who was only ten years older than me. Last year he'd become the first ever Colored photographer for *Life* magazine. We were a decade or so removed from the Harlem Renaissance; and it was a pleasure and proof that our artistic greatness survived its waning.

"Enough stalling, Miss Lady. Get to painting."

I gathered charcoal pencils to sketch an outline before sitting at my easel. Glancing back and forth from the photograph to the canvas, I dared myself to paint an even more lifelike rendition of the two friends. A sensation, both calming and thrilling, coursed through me as I propped the photograph on the side table and readied my heart for creation.

Landscapes and nature were once my forte, but portraits and renderings of the beauty of those about me captivated my fascination a few years prior to college. That fascination was only enhanced by the celebration of Negro life seen in the works studied during my undergraduate education. Human forms had dominated my artistry ever since.

I paused to take in the paintings I'd completed that now lined the shelves, hung on walls, or rested my rear workbench. Black, brown, redbone, or cafe au lait, my paintings showcased Colored folks, particularly women, in our glory. These were my contributions to our exquisite beauty.

"Afternoon, Miz Jackson."

Mr. Lyman's booming voice interrupted my intent.

He's at the Jacksons'!

I dropped the charcoal pencil in its box and raced from the shed in my haste to reach the postman.

My student, Suda Mae Jackson, and her family lived two doors down. By the time I reached the mailbox in front of our house, Mr. Lyman had barely cleared the Jacksons' front yard. That meant I had to wait for him to finish a conversation with our immediate neighbor next door.

Lord, don't let Mr. Cheathom have one of his talking frenzies.

Our dear next door neighbor was in his mid-eighties and prone to repeating himself multiple times in the simplest sentences. He must've been tired because he merely took the mail, waved at me, and slowly ambled back onto his front porch where he tossed his mail on a chair before sitting and folding his hands in his lap, ready for his afternoon siesta.

That freed Mr. Lyman to head in my direction.

"Afternoon, Miss Ilona. How's everybody? Miz Maple? Mr. Jonah?"

"Mother and Father are resting, and they're fine. Thank you for asking."

"Good to hear. Miz Grayson down at the mercantile sends her apologies. She found these here envelopes in one of her candy barrels. Guess they got pushed off the counter and fell in." He raised one of the envelopes toward the sun and squinted as if his spectacles were malfunctioning. "Looking at this postmark, I'd say they been in there a good while."

He handed me the mail and continued chattering. "That's why these city townsmen need to hurry up and get us on task for a real, honest to God federal post office instead of using the mercantile. Now, don't make no mistakes, I like my job. But it ain't got no real benefits without that federal designation. Lessen you counts chatting with ladies as lovely as you on a regular basis."

"Thank you, Mr. Lyman. For the mail. And the compliment." Might've been rude of me not to further engage in pleasantries, but I needed the postman to move on with his duties so I could run to my art shed and privately scour the mail.

Lord, please let it be here!

I hurried toward the backyard, catching in my peripheral vision yet ignoring the abandoned outhouse at the edge of our property that Mother had repeatedly asked Father to raze only for it to become a forgotten eyesore after his illness. It was an eyesore worth forgetting.

Closing the door of my art shed, I leaned against it to catch my breath before quickly shuffling through the small stack of mail.

My heart pounded rapidly at sight of a long-awaited, officious looking envelope.

"Oh, dear God..."

I stood there staring at the envelope that held my hopes. Its corners were crinkled and creased as if the missive had endured an arduous journey or it had been abused in Miz Grayson's candy bins. Still, the envelope was beyond precious, so important to me that it fluttered in the palm of my hand I couldn't keep from trembling.

The Nubian-Kush Art Collaborative.

I read and reread the New York return address, willing this not to be a trick.

The Nubian-Kush Art Collaborative received funding from the Federal Arts Project, philanthropic patrons, and some of the world's leading Negro artists. It provided sponsorship and opportunities to study art here and abroad, to further hone one's skills under the tutelage of master craftsmen and women. The work fellows produced during their fellowship or residency was displayed in exhibits and art installations hosted by major museums. The award included housing, a monetary stipend, and wasn't merely prestigious. The experience allowed exposure and opportunities that persons who looked like me might otherwise be denied in the art world, as well as supportive camaraderie and the building of lasting relationships.

I stared at the return address, noting that the organization's name seemingly pulsed with magnetic energy. I closed my eyes and pressed the envelope to my chest, afraid to open it.

I can't do it. What if it's a rejection?

Sudden sensations of last night, being with Willard and his suppression—forbidding any culmination of what my body was feeling—welled up in me. I was well-versed in rejection. The collaborative's possible denial wouldn't break me if Willard's hadn't.

"But I can't do it here."

The persons I lived with would frown upon my applying for, let alone being accepted into, an arts fellowship.

If you got in.

Stuffing the envelope in my pocket, I raced indoors to make sure my parents were still napping before grabbing the old bicycle I rarely used that was parked outside of my art shed. Hopping on, I wobbled a bit before regaining my balance and peddling like the wind toward the home of Greenie Bruce Simpson, my forever confidant and dearest friend.

Five

"Come on, Ilona! You gonna make me pee waiting on you to open the doggone thing."

"Greenie, I can't! I'm too nervous." I paced a full circle around one of the raised planter boxes in my dearest friend's greenhouse, trying to deplete nervous energy not exhausted on the bike ride here. One of the only Colored female farmers in the region, the greenhouse was to my beloved Greenie what my art shed was to me: her everything. When arriving, I'd gone straight to the greenhouse, knowing where she'd be when not finding her in her rows upon rows of neatly planted fields.

"Fine. Give it here." She snatched the envelope from my hands and tore it open, rapidly extracting a folded sheet of paper the toasty color of butter pecan ice cream. She shook it to release its folds only for me to snatch it back.

"Greenie, wait. What if I didn't get into the program?"

"What if you did?"

I stared into her big, brown eyes, admiring their luminous clarity as if for the first time.

They were seductive with their upturned corners, what

some folks called "bedroom eyes" with their ability to enchant and mesmerize. According to Greenie, they were her only redeeming feature—that and her ability to make anything grow from God's green earth. Naturally, I disagreed. Even in her denim overalls, well-worn brogans, tattered straw hat, and soil-smudged shirt, Clementine "Greenie" Bruce Simpson was gorgeous to me.

"If I did get in...I risk angering Mother and Father...and Willard."

"Honey, they been mad before and anger ain't killed none of 'em yet."

An image of my father, wheelchair bound and essentially defenseless, flashed through my mind.

It almost did.

"They'll get over it," Greenie continued, obviously forgetting how defying my parents and forsaking the pursuit of an honorable degree in English caused my father's condition. But then again, she held the opinion that my actions hadn't contributed to Father's illness. Life, age, and his own stubbornness had. "I love your parents like my own but, girl, you're grown."

"I know that, Greenie, but Willard—"

"Needs to be supportive of you the same as you are of him."

I tucked my chin to my chest and looked at the only person with whom I'd dared to subvert a Christian wife's duty of suffering silently and confided my husband's true nature. "Are we talking about the same individual? Willard Eugene Brinks? Supportive?"

She laughed. "One can wish. Now, quit stalling. My heirloom tomatoes'll ripen before you get this letter finished."

"It's autumn. Not spring. You haven't even planted them yet."

"Precisely."

I stuck my tongue at her, took a deep breath, and smoothed out the paper. "Okay. Let's read it. *Together.*"

We read aloud, our voices rising in unified excitement when reaching the second sentence.

"It is with greatest pleasure that we extend a provisional offer of acceptance into our one-year art fellowship program…"

Ecstatic squeals erupted from our lips. I dropped the letter on a nearby potting table and grabbed Greenie, hugging her fiercely.

"I knew it, Ilona! I told you you'd get in!"

And she had, encouraging me when I'd secretly submitted the application and its ten dollar application fee four months ago despite my concerns and hesitations. Checking the mailbox was solely my responsibility; still, I found myself rushing outdoors to intercept Mr. Lyman on his deliveries, heart clamoring in my chest, afraid my family might develop a sudden interest in collecting the mail and discover my deceit. Hallelujah, they hadn't.

"How do you feel?"

"Amazingly blessed!" I gripped her hands and twirled in a circle as if we were still children playing Ring Around the Rosie on summer days drenched in sunshine and the flitting of butterflies.

We giggled breathlessly when finished.

I opened my mouth to offer heavenly praise, but my joy faded and mirth was suddenly short-lived. "What do they mean by provisional offer?"

I grabbed the letter and read it quickly but carefully in its entirety.

The paper sagged in my grip when I finished, as if embodying my disappointment. "I have to appear in person."

My application had included letters of recommendation from my former professors, a reproduced collage of my work, and an art review from the exhibit I'd created at Fisk as part of my graduation project. Apparently, that was insufficient. Now, I was to do an in-person presentation in order for the admissions committee to make a final decision.

I gave Greenie the letter, allowing her to read it, after which she smiled brightly. "But this is good, girl! The only provisional thing is your actual placement."

Apparently, my work and that of another artist was under consideration for the senior artist-in-residency position. This final step of the process was both crucial and necessary.

"LoLo, I don't see a problem." Greenie reverted to the nickname she'd given me. "They were nice enough to give you two options. The committee's convening in Raleigh. That ain't but a hop, skip, and jump away. If you don't wanna do that, you can travel to New York one of the other times listed in the letter to meet with them. Whatta you think is best?"

"Raleigh, of course. It's much closer than New York."

"I agree. I don't see a problem, but your face is looking like one exists."

I exhaled and smiled slightly before pointing out the specified dates. "They'll be in Raleigh for two days only... Oh great goodness!"

"*What*?"

I held the letter up in front of her. "It's *next* weekend."

"What kinda nonsense? Folks ain't never heard of giving a body advance notice?"

I repeated Mr. Lyman's explanation and apology.

Greenie whistled while shaking her head. "I swear. Miz Grayson needs to quit running her mouth and being all up in her customers' business and pay attention to getting the mail properly distributed."

Nervously, I played with the hair at the nape of my neck. "Greenie, this meeting is too soon. I can't get away that quickly. I can't get away, period."

"Yes, you can." She pulled my hand away from my hair and squeezed it reassuringly. "If you need help with a bus ticket or train fare—"

"I need help with Willard." My husband was tolerant of my art, not supportive. Despite our meeting while in college and his full awareness of what my gift meant to me, he treated it like a bored housewife's indulgence. He was indifferent. Dismissive. My traveling out of town to present work for which he held no regard would be met with his full, characteristic objection.

Not to mention that of my parents.

I needlessly laid it out for Greenie despite her being well versed in the dynamics of my familial relationships. "I can't expect favorable responses from them on a regular basis. They're gonna definitely be bent outta shape about not being aware of the fellowship or that I applied in the first place."

Her lips curved upward. "That was your best move to date."

I couldn't help mirroring her smile, feeling a bit triumphant.

I'd been sneaky. Secretive. So had my sister, Ravena, who was twelve years my senior. My parents' only unmarried daughter, Ravena, was the brave one who'd left Colemanville to chase her dream of writing. She had bumps and bruises that proved her path wasn't easy, but she'd paid her dues and had been blessed in ways that made her sacrifices worthwhile. Now, she was the principal writer for one of the nation's oldest Colored newspapers in Philadelphia. She was the one responsible for my subterfuge. Had she never mailed me the page from her newspaper's culture and arts section containing the advertisement for the art program, I'd have never known about it. I was immensely grateful that she had.

If anyone can do this, you can.

Ravena had circled the advertisement in red and included that handwritten opinion in the margin.

Greenie had agreed, periodically pausing her own duties to check in at my art shed and make sure I was accomplishing the tasks needed for the application process.

It felt like a covert operation, secretly soliciting recommendation letters and preparing my collage. It was the one time Willard's disinterest worked to my benefit.

I could count on three fingers the number of times he'd stepped into my art shed and still have fingers to spare. As for Mother, she was too preoccupied with Father's health to demonstrate interest in my art that she'd dubbed my "little rebellion." Their oblivion allowed me to successfully apply without detection.

"Yeah...well, Greenie...like your mother likes to tease, we're a pair of miscreants needing an extra dose of communion."

Her laughter filled the space. "Maybe. For real, LoLo, do you need help with a train ticket?"

I'd withdrawn the ten dollar application fee from the small box I kept hidden in my lingerie drawer, in which I stashed the allowance Willard gave me from my earnings. The box contained feminine monthly sanitary needs. Even if Willard ever came across it, that box would certainly remain untouched. Few things could make my husband more squeamish than the mere mention of anything pertaining to monthly flows and female issues.

"No, honey, I'm sure I have more than enough." I'd never take money from Greenie knowing how hard she worked to keep her farm profitable year to year. "But you can put your devious mind to work helping me think of a way to get to Raleigh next weekend."

Our laughter floated upward, light as clouds in the autumn sky.

"We have the DOLLs meeting."

The DOLLs–Daughters of Legacy and Light–was Colemanville's women's auxiliary committee composed of the female descendants of the town's founding fathers. Our work was community-minded. Clothing drives. Food pantry. Sewing circle and blanket making. Organization of the Annual Homecoming Day celebration and Juneteenth. Charm classes. Visiting the sick and shut in. And other such activities of self-sufficiency and communal uplift.

Greenie self-corrected. "Never mind. Our meetings are on Fridays. Not Saturday."

"Thank God it's Saturday and won't interfere with the Harvest Festival come Monday."

"You love those kids."

I definitely did. Each year I volunteered to help with the festival in some capacity, usually something that proved hands-on with the children. I adored little ones and wanted several of my own, but no time soon. Not until Willard and I were on better footing financially, and my art had a chance to become whatever it was destined to be.

Something deliciously naughty stole over me. "Greenie, wait! What about your farmers' meeting? Isn't it in Durham next weekend?"

She frowned, not grasping my devious line of thinking. "Yes. And?"

"Have you decided if you're attending?"

Her big lovely eyes widened slowly. "If I do, you're going with me?"

I nodded. "At least that's the story I'm telling." I conveyed my thoughts rapidly. Breathlessly.

Once the train had taken us far enough out of town to safely execute my duplicity, we'd go our separate ways—Greenie to the Colored Farmers' of America quarterly meeting, me to Raleigh and the arts committee.

"Oooh, LoLo! My granny always said it's the quiet ones

you gotta watch. That's downright wicked and I *love* it!" Greenie grabbed my hand and rushed us outdoors, chattering in nonstop excitement as we headed toward her home with its quaint, farmhouse charm.

Am I really about to do this?

The notion felt luscious. Risky. I smiled the entire time Greenie searched for her meeting materials, thinking that ten dollar application fee might have been a sacrifice, but it was the best money I'd ever spent. And it hadn't been frivolous. It was an investment in myself. Even if it was clandestine.

I'm going to Raleigh next week. I will be bold and stand before that committee to present my work with God-given confidence.

Such was my repeated recitation as I pedaled toward home, nervous but exhilarated.

"I'm a fully grown woman and shouldn't have to *ask* Willard or my parents' permission for anything."

I deserved time, space, and opportunity to immerse myself in my gifting and all that it offered despite their limiting mindsets and objections.

My heart experienced a little ping of disappointment, a longing for their support, their belief in me. That had yet to be my experience. And I wanted it. I let myself imagine that Willard's day had gone so wonderfully that he'd surprise the shoes off of my feet by agreeing that my going to Raleigh was, indeed, a good thing.

"That'll happen when Pumpkin Minkins stops stealing other women's men."

I laughed before chiding myself for uncharitable opinions.

I'm going to Raleigh next week. I will be bold and stand before that committee...

I forgot about Pumpkin and resumed my recitation, letting it fill me with courage. The more I recited, the faster I pedaled, fueled by the power of hope and optimism. The faster I pedaled, the more I felt as if I were flying on the wings of all the glorious possibilities Colored women merited but didn't receive.

"We deserve good things!"

I released the handlebars and tossed my head back with a pure sensation of freedom that lasted a mere moment.

Freedom was interrupted by a loud hiss. My eyes snapped open.

On the otherwise deserted road in front of me was a black cat, back arched, seemingly frozen. A horn honked behind me as I swerved to avoid the feline that suddenly came to life and ran directly across my path again as if it was confused or on a mission to complicate my passage.

I jerked the handlebars left only for the front wheel to pitch into a dip in the road. My bike careened dangerously from my overcorrecting. That combined with the speed I'd been traveling, sent me airborne like a chicken with no wings.

I nearly passed out from the impact of my head slamming against the hard packed dirt beneath me.

"Ilona!"

The sound of running feet engulfed me as I lay, eyes closed, unable to move courtesy of the blinding pain stomping about my skull.

"Don't move! Stay still."

I obeyed the voice above me, wishing death to every cat in Colemanville.

Perhaps I passed out. Or maybe it was merely the sensation of a strong grip about me, hoisting me upward that had me feeling as if I were floating in a gentle dream.

There was no need to open my eyes. I knew the touch of

the one who carried me. I simply rested my throbbing head against his chest and slowly inhaled the familiar, soothing scent of Gabe Thurman.

Six

"How many fingers am I holding up, Ilona?"

"Three."

"What letters come before and after M?"

"L and N."

"What day is it?"

"Wednesday."

"The *date*, Ilona?"

"Move, Gabe."

Seated on the open tailgate of his faithful truck, Big Blue, I pushed against the wide wall of Gabe's chest, wishing he was soft and pliable like Willard. Not hard-bodied and unyielding.

He ignored my command and examined the side of my head with gentle, expert fingers as if Doc Everett, Flo's father, planned to anoint him successor of his medical practice. "You have a goose egg."

"Thanks, Dr. Thurman. Will I live?" I snickered softly as if I'd gotten into Willard's secret bottle of Wild Turkey stashed beneath the bathroom sink that he didn't know I knew he possessed.

"I find nothing funny 'bout what just happened."

"I'm the one a cat tried to kill, so neither do I, Gabriel."

He frowned before continuing. "Forget a cat! I coulda run you over, coming around that blind bend in the road, if I hadn't been watching carefully."

I stiffened a bit, feeling scolded. I pushed away a bristling sensation and told myself to act like a civilized Christian woman. "Thank God you're a conscientious driver or that black cat coulda caused us seven years of bad luck."

He scowled, clearly concerned my insignificant head injury was more severe than initially perceived. "I'm not for superstition, but that bad luck nonsense applies to broken mirrors. Not felines."

"What about broken hearts and broken dreams?" Clearly, I'd jarred my good sense on impact. I rushed ahead, embarrassed by speaking so loosely. "I appreciate you for going out of your way...you know...for stopping and helping me."

He grunted the same as he had yesterday when annoyed by Pumpkin Minkins.

I greatly disliked the notion of occupying the same space as an inappropriately friendly woman like Pumpkin and decided to hush and let him finish whatever medical assistance he thought he was giving.

"Sit still while I get my canteen and fish out a bandage."

"For what?"

"That." He nodded toward rivulets of blood sliding down my right arm where it had been scraped raw.

"Oh, good God..." Pain shot across my arm as I twisted it to better view the injury. It wasn't horrific, but it was ugly. Cut. Grubby from gravel and road debris.

I did my best to carefully remove tiny gravel bits while Gabe made quick work of his business. I hadn't accomplished much by the time he returned with a balled up cloth and a sizable canteen.

"Give it here, Ilona. Lemme see."

I extended my injured appendage, not truly feeling the pain. I was too fascinated watching him secure the canteen against his chest with what remained of his right arm before unscrewing its cap with his left hand. I shivered when he slid his amputated limb beneath my injured arm to hold it upright as he poured water, cleaning it with a deft ease I found amazing.

He paused the slightest bit. "You got inquiries?"

"Pardon?"

He stopped his ministrations and locked his honey-colored eyes with mine. "What do you wanna know about it, Ilona?" His voice was hard. Puzzling. "Ask your questions."

When he touched you, you shivered. He misinterpreted that as revulsion.

I opened my mouth to tell him mine was a natural response to missing the tenderness of his touch but good sense kicked in and I opted on the inane instead. "I apologize for getting blood on your shirt. It must've happened when you lifted me. May I take it home and launder it? I'll be sure to return it to you."

He stared at me a moment before shaking his head in a manner that indicated annoyance at my babbling. "I'll take these blood stains any day over what I saw on the battlefield."

"What did you encounter, Gabriel?" Mine was a whispered plea for knowledge, an invitation to lay his burdens down if he so dared. I suddenly ached to know his every experience. And why he failed to come home after the war ended.

And why he left me heartbroken...and subject to Willard.

"What did I encounter?" His voice was steely when echoing my question. "Nothing you wanna see in this life or the next."

He grabbed the cloth he'd placed on the bed of Big Blue, clamped one end between his teeth, and gripped the other with his hand, ripping it mercilessly. Repeatedly. His actions were intense as he made ragged cloth strips I presumed would serve as bandages.

I dared to touch him, gently placing a hand on his and calming his harried movements.

"May I?"

We waited that way, in a frozen tableau, until he finally nodded and released the cloth.

Placing the fabric and its uneven strips on my lap, I put aside any need for medical attention. I took his hand and held it, soothed by the familiar feel of his skin. I closed my eyes as the mere contact of his hand unlatched an internal hinge, sending something both sweet and frightening rolling through me. It was peace. Joy in his presence, a pleasure I hadn't experienced in too many years. The delight was bittersweet. Consuming.

I wanted to, but could neither find nor release words to express the longing for the mutual love we once shared but lost. I honored his service instead.

"Thank you, sir...for fighting for our freedom."

He stared at me, saying nothing as I held his hand, unconsciously stroking it. Admiring its strength. And his.

Looking into his eyes I was hit by the ridiculousness of our situation, that a dusty road, cat-induced, bloodied appendage provided the canvas of our official reunion. I was embarrassed by my failure, as well as his, to connect prior to this.

I'd tried and failed to breach the gap between us. That task was far easier said than done. More than once I'd started in the direction of his family's business in hopes of finding him there, only for nerves and propriety to kick in.

"Nearly six years..."

My feather soft words were barely more than a whisper as I considered the long stretch of time separating us.

He'd enlisted in the army and left in December 1943—the year before I finished college—bound for Germany. I spent that first year after his departure furiously penning letters to him. Praying for his safety and wellbeing. Sending colorful recounts of college life along with love, care packages, and a host of sentiments. I vowed to wait, to be wherever he was when that dreadful, senseless war ended. But he was injured, and the letters he sent me stopped coming. His letters were customarily delayed due to having to cross the wide ocean, and I'd grown accustomed to wanting and waiting. But impatiently, repeatedly waiting during mail calls in the main lobby of my college dormitory resulted in nothing except heartache, worry, and confusion.

When phoning home, making inquiries of them, my parents were tight-lipped. They'd never favored Gabriel. His being a woodworker was somehow unacceptable in their college-degree-having opinions, despite the fact that the Thurman family owned Colemanville's one and only furniture business.

The Thurmans were kind, generous, successful in their own right, what my grandparents called salt of the earth people. Such virtues held little weight with my parents and couldn't stand up against their old school preaching of racial uplift via social standing and advanced education. Gabriel, and his older brother Budd, being the first in their family to finish high school wasn't a cause for celebration in my parents' opinion. A mere high school diploma made him undesirable, an unsuitable match for the youngest daughter of former school superintendent Jonah Robertson. Gabe's sudden disappearance and lack of communication, to them, was a godsend.

Lord, forgive me but my parents are snobs. Acting as if they ain't but one generation removed from slavery.

Those thoughts left quicker than they came. I had no space for them. My heart and head were needed for the man I'd cherished, who'd been swallowed by a war only to resurface.

"Hold your arm up."

I complied, allowing Gabe to wash my wound until satisfactorily clean. Again, I sat entranced watching as he worked with one of the strips of cloth we'd created, anchoring an end between his teeth while wrapping it about my injury. He expertly tucked the end of the strip beneath the bandage in a way that felt as if he'd done so before. Perhaps in the war?

I ignored the sweet sensation of his touch against my arm. "Did you learn that on the battlefield?"

"Maybe."

I continued without thinking. "Why do you avoid me?"

His gaze was warm, locked with mine. "That's a self-answering question, *Miz Brinks*."

I bypassed the rationale in his response, suddenly and perhaps unduly irritated by what felt like his nonchalance. "You've been home three months and this is the first time we've been alone in each other's company. That hurts nearly as much as you disappearing."

He'd returned without a hero's welcome or fanfare. For years he'd been absent and far from here. One day, without warning, he was home, sending my heart and mind in tailspins. But by then I was a married woman unable to express my truest joy at his return. I could only watch, and want, from a distance. If ever a chance encounter occurred, our interactions were intentionally brief and unnaturally stilted. We were cordial. Formal. I hated that I'd never worked up the courage to openly speak with or even confront him. In some ways it felt as if he wasn't here and had simply dissolved into the tapestry that was Colemanville.

He opened his mouth, but closed it quickly and stared into the distance. "Disappearing was for the best."

"How can you say something like that?" I hopped down from the truck bed so suddenly he had to step back. "I received no letters from you for...what? Two? Three? No, *four years*? I never held that against you even though it hurt something fierce." I poked him in the chest. "Then when you do bother coming back to Colemanville it's without me knowing a thing. I find you sitting in the church house one Sunday like you ain't never left. And here I am still in the dark as to why you gave up on us!"

"This ain't enough?" He lifted his abbreviated limb as if it answered all questions.

"Don't you dare use your injury as a reason for failing to return human kindness, Gabriel Thurman! I baked you a strawberry pound cake when you got back and delivered it fresh to your mother's doorstep. I didn't even let it sit overnight before glazing it like I should have—"

"*A cake?* You hot in the jaw over a damn cake and some glaze, Ilona Ann?"

What I was, was disoriented by the cluttered emotions erupting out of me. Raw feelings had me hopping from one topic to the next as tears I refused to let fall burned the back of my eyes. Or perhaps it was the bump on the side of my head that gave me a sensation of swimming but sinking beneath waters I could no longer tread.

"It wasn't just a cake, Gabe! It was your favorite...and the welcome home you deserved but wouldn't dare accept any other way. It was all I could reasonably offer and you never even said thanks! Did the war siphon off your good manners? Or did it simply turn you into a coward?"

My mouth clamped shut, knowing I'd said too much. I stared up at him wanting to retrieve the ugliness I'd unleashed in our atmosphere. I wanted to touch him, to apologize for speaking out of turn and so irrationally only to be caught off guard by his response.

He grinned slowly before releasing that wide, untamed laugh of his I didn't realize I missed. "Nice to know my Sweet Rivers still run deep."

My intrinsic quietness never fully disappeared in Gabe's presence during our courtship. It never needed to. I treasured the freedom he offered, my ability to be quiet yet expressive those precious times we were together. He offered room and space, valued the softness of my personality even while urging and encouraging my honesty. In my art. My thoughts. My feelings. He'd named me his Sweet Rivers—gentle on top, flowing underneath. He honored that complexity, allowing me to be me.

"I was afraid he might've changed you." His voice housed dread and vexation, prompted by my union to Willard Brinks.

"I'm still the same." My words were a gentle breath, a plea for acceptance. I remained where I was, closer to him than was decent, wishing heaven would look away and allow me to truly touch him. But my want was sinful. Nothing heaven could uphold.

Still, it was indisputably lovely being in his presence and feeling as if I lolled beneath the protective shade of a towering tree. My thoughts were odd as I looked up at him.

With Gabriel, there was no need to wear low, square-heeled sensible shoes like white-gloved ushers on Sundays. I could stretch to my full height versus rounding my shoulders and making myself small as I did with Willard.

With Gabe I could be a whole woman.

I suddenly wanted to experience and know such wholeness. But the cost was too great: a ruined marriage.

"Don't ever change, Sweet Rivers. Not for him. Or anybody." He touched my chin lightly, sending shivers through me. "You're perfect as is."

"I don't believe in perfection."

"Same as I don't believe in superstitions. But the one about black cats can't be true seeing as how one ornery cat allowed me to touch you again. Never thought that would happen..."

His voice trailed off in embarrassment or regret. I wasn't certain. All I knew was I needed more of him at that moment. Reaching up, I cupped his face.

He backed away. "Don't start nothing neither of us can finish, Sweet Rivers. You have a husband and I ain't him."

Perhaps it was the throbbing of the knot on the side of my head or the thrill of being an arts scholarship finalist amping up my boldness, but I elevated on my tiptoes before good sense could catch up with me and kissed his cheek. Softly, tenderly. Before he could stop me I moved to those full lips of his and kissed him gently but deeply.

I pressed my body against his, ignoring his unnatural stiffness. His body heat flowed through the fabric of my clothing, yet he stood there rigid and unyielding without reciprocating my misguided longings.

I ended the kiss as swiftly as it began, feeling demoralized. Rejected. "Forgive me for doing that." I turned away, ready to grab my bicycle and pedal away my shame.

"Ilona–"

The sound of a car approaching, horn honking loudly, obnoxiously, suspended whatever his intentions of pacification might have been.

The driver halted the car mere feet away and hopped out, her perfume hitting my nose like a fist despite the distance. She rushed toward us, hips switching, skirt so tight the fabric was loudly protesting.

Lord, we didn't need additional help but if we did, You couldn't send somebody besides Pumpkin Minkins?

Seven

"Dear God, Jesus, and Judas, Gator! You're bleeding, baby." Pumpkin's car had barely rocked to a standstill before she was rushing over like a Negro Nurse Nightingale. With, as Greenie would say, all the grace of a cow in a corset, she knocked me out of her way and promptly laid unholy hands on Gabe. She prodded his chest, his arms, his stomach, and whatever else her hands could reach, patting for nonexistent injuries. "What in the devil happened?"

Gabe stepped aside, ending her unlicensed examination. "I'm fine. Thank you. Ms. Ilona's the one injured."

"Hello, Pumpkin."

She looked at me and shrank backwards, obviously disgusted by my appearance. "Eww, *girl*! You're an unnatural mess. What's wrong with your arm? And your head? You need to go home and get presentable and stop shaming yourself."

Pamela Sue "Pumpkin" Minkins hadn't spoken a kind word to me since I was crowned the Belle of the Christmas Ball in eighth grade. Pumpkin and I were tied for first place and it all came down to a talent showcase. I painted a beautiful watercolor portrait of a hummingbird in less than ten minutes in front of an audience while on stage. Pumpkin danced and sang some song I couldn't rightly recall, but neither gifting proved her forte. When she protested the outcome, a couple of kids our age booed her off the stage. She'd hated me ever since.

"I agree with getting Ms. Ilona home...*to make sure she's okay.*" Gabe gave her a stony glare before lifting my bike onto the bed of Big Blue and closing the tailgate. "Ms. Ilona, you ready?"

"No...no, sir...don't trouble yourself." I politely declined, very aware of Pumpkin's unblinking inspection. "I can make the ride home just fine."

"Clearly you didn't see your bike's a bit on the busted side. You must've hit a pothole or something during your accident. That front tire frame's wobbling outta alignment." He held my elbow and escorted me to Big Blue's passenger door as if minor injuries prevented me from managing safely. "Ms. Pumpkin, if you don't mind, I'ma head on and get Ms. Ilona home to her husband."

She leaned a healthy hip against Gabe's truck, batting her eyelashes and pursing her lips all coquettish. "When you finish, come on by for some oxtails and black eyed peas if you like. Oh, and rice. I made the dirty kind."

If lusty looks created real heat, Gabe would've been incinerated.

"That's kind of you, ma'am. Maybe some other time."

He was behind the wheel within seconds even though it felt like a lifetime to me after witnessing the unmasked appetite of Pumpkin and her relentless ogling.

I told myself jealousy wasn't a virtue as Gabe honked the horn and pulled away. That caution didn't keep me from feeling what I did, or knowing what I perceived. I glanced in the door's side mirror to find her staring; her expression both greedy and cunning.

That woman wants him like a fat man wants cornbread.

Riding home with Gabe was tortuous yet delicious. Sitting quietly in his presence I was struck again by the distance of time and situation between us, and the passing of years since the demise, as well as the origins, of our romance.

It was all by chance.

If Packer had been at school that day, perhaps our attraction would have failed to breathe its first breath. But Packer's family had been in Florida attending a ceremony honoring their Seminole ancestors. His absence gave opportunity to our existence.

I guess I can make do with you.

I smiled at the memory of Gabe's surly capitulation that spring day of eleventh grade as I stared out of Big Blue's window at the passing scenery. We'd grown up together and were friends of a sort, but had no interest in one another until the day he chose me as his partner on a class assignment because of Packer's absence. I remembered sassing back, telling him I'd rather not work with someone whose skills were barely as good as a three-legged possum's with two of those legs tied behind its back. That terminated his bad attitude and made him release that wide, untamed laugh.

"Well, looka here! The little church mouse has a whip for a tongue and can speak for herself."

"And I'll use this tongue to whip you every time you get out of line. Which, knowing you, will be often and'll leave my tongue bruised and tired."

I'd resumed my quiet composure after that, but a surprising attraction between us proved instantaneous. We wound up working well together on that assignment of synchronicity. We were to bring two separate mediums into one harmonious creation—literary, musical, artistic, or scientific. The process was up to us. I was an artist. Gabe was a woodworker. We chose to meld our talents by creating a small wooden box displaying his intricate carvings on its sides and my painting on the hinged lid that Gabe expertly created and attached.

Our beautiful hummingbird box was the beginning...

Despite my parents being less than sanguine about it, our relationship lasted from high school until he failed to return from the war. He claimed to like my quiet nature, my artistic gifts. I was smitten by his gentle smile and boyish charm, and admired his ability to take a hunk of wood and shape it into art. Our relationship had been a symbiotic affair, and even though it suffered a painful death, I'd been unable to part with the box that brought us together, rather keeping it in my art shed storing photographs.

"What're you thinking?"

I was brought back to the present as the sweet flow of my thoughts were interrupted by his question. I shifted my gaze from the passing scenery to glance in his direction. "Nothing."

It was a falsification I'd have to repent for later.

He was quiet before responding. "I know you, Sweet Rivers. You're thinking on something."

I reached for anything, no matter how irrational, to avoid truth and the longings my voyage down memory lane had me suddenly experiencing. "Are you interested in Pumpkin?"

"Pumpkin? *Minkins*?"

"Is there another one in Colemanville?"

He looked at me before laughing as if I'd lost my good sense. "I'm about as interested in her as I am in having you drill a hole in my head with one of your paint brushes sharpened at the end."

"She's interested in you."

He snorted dismissively. "I have no time for women. I'm busy."

"With what?"

"Living." His one-word response housed finality, as if he would never again in life have room or space for matters of the heart.

"Life makes room for love, Gabriel."

"Yeah, and the minute you get comfortable it'll evict you from the rooms you thought you inhabited. Next thing you know you're living outdoors. By your lonesome."

I was certain he referred to our relationship and wanted to challenge that notion, to tell him I never evicted him. He was the one who failed to return to us, to Colemanville. I opened my mouth, ready to unleash a fusillade in my defense, only for him to turn onto the street where I lived.

My parents' house wasn't far ahead.

"I appreciate the ride. You can pull over here." I suddenly wanted to be anywhere he and his false accusations weren't. Neither was I in the mood to endure my parents' scrutiny and disdain if he were to deliver me to our house properly.

When life caught Gabe and I and threw us into love, my parents immediately made their disfavor known. Perhaps because of age and being tired after raising four daughters before me, they gradually grew quiet on the subject. Tolerated it. It wasn't until later that I learned they assumed my affection for Gabe would die a quick death once I went to college. It didn't, and they refused to accept, in their misguided opinions, my settling for what was beneath me. Even now, after Willard and so much water under the bridge, they remained less than cordial toward him and most times barely managed to veil their contempt.

Sometimes their contempt feels like fear.

Perhaps, unlike Willard who said he wanted a place for

ourselves but seemed content living with my parents, they'd objected to Gabe, knowing they couldn't dominate him and feared he would somehow take me from them.

I pushed that baseless thought aside, realizing Gabe was still driving. "You don't have to take me to my house. I can get my bike there without help. I'm close enough to walk."

He ignored me as if I'd said nothing.

"Gabe--"

"What's wrong, Ilona? You ashamed to be seen with the one-armed man?"

I was so taken aback that words couldn't find their way into my mind or my mouth. I sat in silence, disgusted and shocked as he brought Big Blue to a halt in front of my parents' house.

He exited the front cab before I could defrost enough to sputter a sound in my defense or take him to task.

I followed suit, exiting Big Blue to watch him quickly lower the tailgate and lift my bicycle to the ground with dexterity and ease. He rolled it toward the gate surrounding my childhood home, ignoring my presence.

"Thank you, sir. I have it from here." My attempts to remove the bike from his grasp were met with steel-like resistance. "Gabe...let go...and thank you *again*."

We must have looked like two juvenile idiots engaged in a tug-of-war over a bike that was no longer fit to ride.

"Ilona!"

I immediately let go of the bike upon seeing Willard rushing down the front porch. Guilt squirmed through me as if I'd been caught in something unseemly. "Willard...you're home already?"

"I have great news that you absolutely must hear!" He paused suddenly, taking in the sight before him. He looked from me to Gabe and back to me, gaze locking onto the makeshift bandage about my arm before scouring my appearance. "What in heaven happened? Your dress is a bloody, unsightly mess."

He stepped back, face twisted with disgust when I stepped toward him, ignoring his exaggeration.

"I had an accident. Mr. Thurman was kind enough to assist me home." I felt duplicitous, as if I'd intentionally kept secrets from my husband. I knew then and there that I needed to tell him about my past with the man wheeling my bike up the walkway, head high, back straighter than a razor blade.

"Yes...certainly...thank you, Mr. Thurman." Willard waved a hand in an absentminded fashion as if all things outside of himself and his interests were inconsequential. "You're free to leave the bike anywhere. Hurry, Ilona. You must hear my news. It's absolutely splendid!"

His nose wrinkled as he took my arm gingerly. Not due to care for my injuries. But to avoid sullying himself as he hurried me up the walkway toward the porch where my father napped in his wheelchair.

I looked over my shoulder, thinking I should thank Gabe for his kindness despite his misconceptions, only to stumble at his expression. A feuding amalgamation of longing, pain, and indifference distorted his countenance. It made my heart ache despite its brief existence.

It was there one moment. Gone the next. Replaced by a mask that descended over his face with rigid insistence. Even so, I wanted to offer what he was due. "Thank you—"

Willard interrupted. "He's already been thanked. I need your attention on what I'm saying."

I looked from Willard back to Gabe, but he had already turned and walked away. Seconds later the sound of Big Blue's engine revving into life shimmied across the air. I wanted to wave goodbye, to call Gabe back so we could make amends and start fresh. But Willard's chatter reminded me I was married. There was no room for new beginnings.

"Ilona, did you hear what I said? Are you even listening?"

I disconnected from sudden, intense longing and gave my husband my attention. "Sorry...what were you saying?"

"Principal North is retiring at the end of next term. I want his job. And you'll need to help me get it."

Eight

I stared at Willard, not comprehending, completely forgetting my intention to disclose my former relationship with Gabriel. My husband had been blessed with his current position a month before we were married and, subsequently, was the newest teacher on staff at Profit Coleman Elementary. Every one of his fellow teachers had seniority. Yet, he considered himself worthy of serving as head of the school despite never holding a leadership position?

My quiet voice grew even quieter than usual as I tactfully attempted to articulate the obvious.

"It's wonderful that Principal North is retiring. He faithfully served our school for decades and provided superior leadership. Now, he can enjoy his golden years." I took a cautious breath. "I imagine our board of education will want to fill his shoes with someone who's equally experienced."

Colemanville was self-governing and fully incorporated with its own three-member board of education. However, of necessity, our schools reported to the main board overseeing all of Onslow County in order to qualify for and receive subsidized funding from the state. That required an adherence to regulations.

Putting an unqualified, inexperienced person in the principal's position won't win us one benefit. It'll jeopardize us.

Willard hadn't grown up here. He was a transplant from Cincinnati and as such perhaps he couldn't fully appreciate the struggles of a Colored township such as Colemanville.

Our town, named for Flo's great grandfather Profit Coleman, was little more than the site of a burned down plantation in 1875 at the time of its inception. Mr. Profit was the son of Liberty and Ebenezer Hollinswood—the white man who owned Hollinswood Plantation where Liberty was enslaved—the same man who sold eleven of her twelve children in punitive controlling acts or to satisfy his debts. The loss of her children broke her soul, but not her spirit. In an act of desperation and defiance she secured passage on the Underground Railroad for young Profit and three of his peers, my grandfather Cain Robertson included. She was determined that, although he was the last of her children to whom she had access, Profit would know freedom.

Lady Liberty, unfortunately, lost her life in the process.

Slavery ended and a decade passed before Profit returned after earning enough to purchase that burned down plantation and its acreage. He and the three boys, now men, built Colemanville in honor of the woman who freed them.

Profit Coleman. Cain Robertson. Greenie's grandfather, Amos Bruce. And Dimple and Zayda's forebear, Isaiah Mosely. These were the founding fathers of Colemanville. A town founded, not merely to honor Liberty, but to allow for the safety, wellness, and economic advancement of the newly freed. Colemanville was insulated, protected by armed men, against lynchings and pogroms of racial violence. It was a quiet place of ownership, not sharecropping, that employed its own sheriff, boasted many businesses, and even a library. That didn't mean protocols could be flaunted as Willard seemingly expected. Colemanville was steeped in its own traditions and orderly decency was one of them.

"Experience is nothing but a euphemism for staid and outdated." Willard was animated, nearly vibrating with stubborn insistence. "What this town and that school needs isn't experience, but vision. I have that!"

I listened intently, growing increasingly horrified as he conveyed a plan for reform involving mandatory student uniforms, tuition-based attendance, and accelerated courses including subjects such as Latin.

"I believe strict discipline produces excellence. Corporal punishment will be reinstated. There will be no bringing lunch to school in grease-stained paper bags or undignified metal buckets. No more *not* bathing every school night. Or other such slovenliness." He frowned as if offended. "Filthy little children mar the Colored race. Cleanliness is next to godliness and hygiene is imperative."

Needing to sit before Willard's pompousness stole my strength, I took the empty chair next to my father who was still napping peacefully with a blanket draping his legs. "True...proper hygiene aids wellness...but *tuition*, Willard?"

"It'll be reasonable. Particularly for families who've procreated like rabbits and have multiple offspring. In such instances, the tuition will be per household. Not per student."

I felt sick to my stomach. "Willard, this is Colemanville. We're a small town with a small population. We're a tight-knit and, in some regards, rather rural community. Why impose big city concepts such as tuition? Depending on the amount, you could conceivably exclude entire families. The less fortunate would be unable to attend."

I was stunned by the nearly villainous smile widening his round face.

"Precisely!" He adjusted his spectacles and cleared his

throat as if preparing for a grand speech. "I plan to reconfigure that pathetic elementary school into Colemanville's first elite institution."

I closed my eyes and silently prayed that God would strike some sense into him as he droned on and on about his intended reformations. Each sounded more heartless than the previous.

"And perfect attendance will be absolutely mandatory."

I shook my head and, again, attempted to be the voice of reason. "Willard, we both know that's impossible. Children get sick—"

"They won't when they adhere to my hygiene regulations."

I continued as if he'd said nothing worth hearing because he hadn't. "Again, Colemanville is *partially* a rural community. Consequently, some families rely on the help of their children to work in the fields. Particularly during harvest season."

He shrugged indifferently. "I suppose they'll have a choice to make. Harvesting. Or learning. And if tuition is the thing that separates the dedicated from the unfaithful, so be it."

"Willard, this plan sounds...absolutely unfair." I thought about Greenie and the times she'd missed school helping her family gather the ripe offerings of the earth. Completing her primary education hadn't been easy, yet she'd done so and gone on to study agriculture at Tuskegee University. Had nonsense such as what Willard proposed existed back then, my best friend might have never completed her primary education and graduated college.

"If life was fair we'd be raising our own family already. That is, if you tried harder to conceive. And we certainly wouldn't be living with your parents." He pushed his glasses higher on his nose and leaned back against the porch railing, resting his weight. "That's another thing. Tuition will supplement and increase the teachers' salaries. And, of course, mine as principal. And, do you know what else I discovered? The house Principal North lives in?" He paused and leaned toward me for dramatic effect. "He doesn't own it. It comes with the position!"

His smile was more of a gloat, as if heaven and fate had predetermined his favorable outcome and he was already celebrating.

"That means it would be just the two of us." He glanced at Father and lowered his voice. "We'd still need to be decent... but we wouldn't have to be as discreet and could better enjoy our marriage bed."

You mean you'd treat me like a real wife and not a mere orifice that takes you to a point where I'm not needed anymore?

I swallowed that without saying anything only for my thoughts to take a sharp, irrational turn and latch onto Gabe. He'd been the first in his family to complete high school. By no means did that make the Thurmans ignorant. They were shrewd, successful business people without formal education whose woodwork and furniture was absolutely exquisite. They were indicative of many others in Colemanville. Listening to Willard, I understood him to be an elitist who would place no value in them.

"This conversation started with you saying I needed to help you get this promotion." I'd had enough and needed a reprieve from my husband's exclusionary elitism and redirected him to his favorite subject: Willard Brinks. "What exactly does that entail?"

"Principal North will, undoubtedly, be the biggest decision maker in choosing his replacement. He's an art lover, and his favorite artist is some fellow named..." He paused, looking into space as if attempting to reclaim missing information. "Harvey Oswald Tanner."

"Henry Ossawa Tanner," I corrected.

He grunted irritably before continuing. "Yes. Perhaps. I'd like to gift one of Tanner's pieces to Principal North."

"Are you saying you want to...*bribe* him?"

"Gift. Bribery. Useless euphemisms, Ilona."

I sat back and breathed calming breaths, wishing I was bold enough to reach over and slap the ignorance out of him.

I'd long been aware of Willard's ambitious, competitive nature and the high hopes he held for his career and future. I'd also caught glimpses of a latent cruelty on occasion; his critical nature and revulsion of others that went beyond snobbery. Still, and shame on me, I found this desire to weasel his way into a position shocking. And definitely disgusting.

"Mr. Tanner is a world-class artist." I tried a more direct tactic to reach Willard's logic: economics. "His pieces are far beyond our budget. We cannot afford any such purchase."

"I said nothing about purchasing an original. You're an artist. Find a photo of one of Tanner's works and replicate it. Including the signature."

I stood so fast my chair wobbled backwards. I grabbed it before it could crash to the porch and awaken my father. I checked to ensure he was still napping before turning on Willard.

I wasn't one to disrespect my husband. And I'd certainly never raised my voice in anger at him, but his suggestion was downright reprehensible. And I was beyond insulted. "If you're suggesting I forge the work of another artist, you've lost whatever good sense you were born with!"

His arm snaked out, his hand gripping my arm so fast, so furiously, that it took a moment for the pain to catch up with his motion. When it did, fire shot through my bandaged, injured arm as he tightly latched onto it.

He leaned in, his face nearly touching mine. "If I can't count on you for this, what good are you to me? You aren't the best artist I've ever seen, but even you can accomplish something as simple as this. If not...I might be forced to consider you useless."

"Is everything alright out here?"

Willard released me instantly at the sound of my mother approaching.

We turned to find her pushing the screen door open and stepping onto the porch.

Willard smiled sweetly. "Of course it is, Mother Robertson. I was just sharing my good news with Ilona."

"Isn't it marvelous, Ilona, dear? Your husband's a rising star. God always favors His chosen."

I stared at my mother, wondering if she'd taken good leave of her senses as well. Or had she fallen victim to Willard's disillusioned spell? Yes, my parents adored my spouse, but Mother was the wife of a former school superintendent. Certainly she understood her son-in-law wasn't qualified for the position.

I suddenly wanted to race indoors to locate the pad and pen Father used to communicate when his speech was too garbled for us to comprehend. I wanted to wake him and ask him to offer a sound perspective capable of overturning such sheer foolishness; no matter how abbreviated or poorly written his compromised penmanship.

"I'll see you both at supper. I have lessons to grade." Willard headed indoors, a jaunty bounce in his normally heavy gait.

Mother followed, chattering happily.

I remained where I was, feeling as if the spirits of Dr. Jekyll *and* Mr. Hyde had possessed my husband.

Slowly, my gaze shifted to my father dozing peacefully.

Father had worked into his early seventies. Mother's running joke had been that only the Grim Reaper could enforce his retirement. Instead, a stroke had. Since then Father's life had been altered by illness, and the bustling, efficient energy he'd once possessed was now severely diminished.

We never should've disagreed about you choosing Willard for me.

Whatever, if any, leniency my parents may have possessed in their younger years was exhausted on my older sisters. With me they weren't strict. They were domineering. Controlling. Authoritative. I lived as if in a fishbowl, under not only their ever watchful gaze, but that of my older siblings as well. I was never coddled, indulged, or babied. I was the last of the Robertson girls and was expected to be a shining representation of our household, and all the good my family had sacrificed for, instilled in, and demanded of me. But I was the one who broke my parents' hearts, stole my father's strength by insisting on loving Gabriel.

Lightly, I touched Father's hand, not wanting to wake him, my heart suddenly heavy with old regret for brazenly defying my parents by insisting on who and what I wanted. Seeing Father's shrunken frame was a reminder that the conflict wasn't worth it. Not when the outcome had been so disastrous.

What about your wants? Your freedom?

Ignoring the thought, I closed my eyes and inhaled the scents of autumn. The spice of a sweet potato pie being baked by one of the neighbors. The clean, sharp notes of pine trees in the distance. The warm, fruitiness of sassafras that Greenie and homegrown botanists harvested for root beer and even toothpaste. These familiar, fragrant comforts soothed my disturbed nerves and cleared my mind with sweet gentleness.

Willard married you for your father's connections.

I sat up straight and looked around, expecting an unseen speaker to appear, the voice had been so distinctively clear. But there was only Father and I.

An icy sensation shivered down my spine, leaving my mind inexplicably filled with that long lived myth of divine intervention.

According to town lore Lady Liberty, Flo's great-great-grandmother who gave her life saving her twelfth child, appeared when little ones needed rescuing from time to time. Always dressed in white. Skirts flowing on a sweet-scented breeze. A heroine and the champion of Colemanville. Lady Liberty.

I wasn't a child, but I suddenly felt as if I was floundering. Hopeless. And helpless. In a loveless, disfigured marriage with a man I realized I didn't fully know or trust. A man willing to use unscrupulous means to get what he wanted. And what he wanted was simple: for nepotism to work in his favor.

Willard Brinks was shrewdly plotting to benefit from his connection to Jonah Robertson, from my father's standing in the community as our town's revered former school superintendent.

I stared at my father, wondering if he would object to Willard's manipulating their relationship for his gain, only to recall that Willard was the chosen. Not Gabe. Father had taken to Willard instantly, claiming to see in him a glimmer of his younger self. Where Father saw familiar ambition, I saw a familiar, unflattering self-righteousness. Now, this son-in-law of his intended to bastardize my artistic skills and create a forgery to aid his greed.

Father got the son he wanted in Willard. And Willard got a boost up the ladder.

I felt misused by both men.

That truth settled its sad sensations inside of me. I inhaled deeply, exhaled completely before lifting my face heavenward and silently offering a simple plea.

Mother Liberty, help me. Please.

NINE

"Ladies, we realize this evening's meeting has lasted well beyond our normal time for adjournment, but next year's annual celebration must be absolutely magnificent. We greatly appreciate your time and patience, and will do our best to be finished within the next few minutes."

I sat with my beloved DOLLs–Greenie, Flo, Zayda, and Dimple–in our weekly meeting hearing yet not hearing Madam Chairperson, my attention fading in and out when I should've been fully present. Our meetings were run with precision and decorum, but they also provided a lovely opportunity for fellowship, feminine empowerment, and sisterhood that I cherished. Customarily, I attended with rapt attention if not wholehearted enthusiasm and participation, but that evening I was distracted when I couldn't afford to be. From now until August of the following year, every DOLLs meeting would hold even more importance as we prepared to celebrate Colemanville's seventy-fifth anniversary.

"Next year's annual homecoming marks Colemanville's jubilee! That's seventy-five years for a town that started with nothing to become something. And that's even more significant if you stop and consider many other Colored towns that are dwindling or have become nonexistent. DOLLs, this *will* be our best celebration yet...even if we have to rob Paul blind and kidnap Peter to do it!"

Vibrant laughter danced about the room in response to Madam Chairperson's passionate pronouncement. The room was full of energy and readiness. We were an army of women prepared to follow our commander and chief into a fabulous fray of baking, cooking, decorating, and organizing in honor of Colemanville's seventy-fifth year of existence; yet, it was as if I wasn't there, my mind was so stretched in various directions.

My husband wants me to forge a painting by a master artist I admire.

I have to falsify my whereabouts to get to Raleigh next weekend.

And I have no right to care, but Gabe's being pursued by Pumpkin.

"Mr. Chairman, I got plenty ideas on how y'all can go about making next year's shindig one to remember. Starting with semi-burlesque dancers. Y'all recall them summers I spent in Chicago? Well, I did a whole heap of singing and dancing, so I gots whatever choreographering is needed."

That foolishness cut through my worried musings, had me looking around the church fellowship hall for the speaker improper enough to make such an outlandish suggestion.

She sat at the rear of the room looking deadly serious.

Pumpkin.

She glanced about, looking from one woman to the next, impressed with herself and the silence her ridiculousness created. Eventually her gaze landed on me. When it did she grinned slowly, like an alley cat who'd caught the prized canary.

"And *that's* why you don't let *everybody* on the premises or in the party."

I pinched Greenie's leg, praying her whisper hadn't been overhead in the shocked silence that held everyone captive until Madam Chairperson delicately cleared her throat releasing us from Pumpkin's spell.

Attendees were suddenly murmuring, sputtering and muttering, and shifting in their seats, clearly outdone by Pumpkin's brazenness.

"DOLLs! Ladies!" Madam Chairperson daintily rapped her gavel atop the table where she sat at the front of the room. "Quiet, please." She waited for compliance before continuing. "Thank you for your input, Miss Minkins. It is duly noted. Howsomever—"

"Wait now. Hold on. If budget's an issue, it shouldn't be 'cause y'all wouldn't even have to pay me. And no need to worry about the routine. Like I said, I know something 'bout choreographering and I'm fully able to handle the whole shebang."

"Just 'cause you're able don't mean you're stable."

I looked over in time to see Flo elbow her cousin, Tippy, seated beside her.

Nineteen, same as Flo, Tippy was a firecracker who never shied away from voicing an opinion. Her barely whispered comeback left Greenie and Miss Zayda covering their mouths with lacy handkerchiefs to muffle their laughter.

"Alright now, Daughters of Legacy and Light...act right." Miss Dimple, Miss Zayda's older sister and the owner of the town's diner, sat with her shapely legs crossed, hands folded in her lap—the picture of female elegance. She was several years older than me. Closer to forty. The sound and sensible one. Same as Flo's dearly departed mother, Iva. Miss Iva Rae Coleman had been to Miss Dimple what Greenie was to me, and she'd been crushed by Miss Iva Rae's passing. Without her sister of the heart, she was the remaining voice of reason in our intimate circle of descendants of the founding fathers of Colemanville. "If that child wants to lead a group of musty armed, ass-shaking females in the name of the town's seventy-fifth birthday I ain't getting in her way. Have at it semi-burlesque, semi-sane."

Dimple's deadpan humor left our group hard-pressed to keep from erupting into full-fledged, belly-aching laughter that would have been highly inappropriate as well as disruptive.

"Yes ma'am, Miss Dimple, and my apologies." Tippy's pretense at repentance was betrayed by the lopsided smirk on her face. She winked when our eyes met and returned her attention to the proceedings.

I love that girl's outspokenness. And her spirit.

Tippy, even Flo for that matter, was younger than me yet both possessed a certain confidence that I considered admirable. Refreshing.

You have power in your voice and the same ability to speak.

That eerie sensation experienced yesterday, after Willard's grand announcement and when sitting with Father as he napped on the front porch, occurred again. Goosebumps marked my arms and I wanted to look around for the voice that had spoken despite knowing no one would be there. Instead, I gave Madam Chairperson my attention as she politely addressed Pumpkin in a way that left no room for further foolishness.

That didn't derail Pumpkin's insistence. "Excuse me, Person Chairman, 'cause I don't attend these little things regularly but I didn't think this was one of them committees where the head person gets to veto everything. Ain't y'all supposed to vote when new ideas come to y'all's attention?"

Madame Chairperson was, thankfully, unflustered and continued with her usual decorum. "Miss Minkins, you're absolutely correct. The DOLLs do adhere to a democratic progress." She smoothed a hand over her impeccable dress as if brushing away nonexistent wrinkles or lint. "Ladies, before us is the newly proposed matter of a..." She paused and cleared her throat. "A...*semi*-burlesque show as entertainment for next year's festival. All in favor, please raise your hands."

Seeing that hers was the only one in the air, Pumpkin jumped to her feet. "I thought y'all was all about womanhood and progress!"

"Ain't nothing new or progressive about hoochie coochies shaking ass for men."

Tippy's quiet commentary left even Miss Dimple covering her mouth to suppress a laugh, and Flo elbowing her cousin yet again. Unfortunately, it wasn't quiet enough for Pumpkin *not* to overhear.

"I suppose y'all cottonheads sitting up there in the poor folks peanut gallery got a better idea?"

Miss Dimple reached across me and grabbed Tippy's arm when she turned to face Pumpkin, mouth ready to say God knew what.

"Actually, Madam Chairperson, if I may?" I was on my feet, hand raised before I knew what *I* was doing.

"Yes, Sister Brinks?"

"I appreciate Ms. Minkins' reminder that we're for womanhood and progress. I understand the desire to showcase our feminine collective. To be seen and not silent." I turned, facing the rear of the room where she stood, and softly continued as if an unexplainable thing had a hold on me. Dance was a beautiful expression and outlet, but I disagreed with it in a manner that was exploitative. "Perhaps, there's a different, more agreeable way to go about that."

"Such as?" Pumpkin spat, arms crossed, hip jutting to one side and looking belligerent.

I glanced at Greenie, wishing I understood what had me in its grip. Greenie merely nodded encouragingly. It wasn't that I was perpetually silent at meetings, but I certainly didn't tangle with outraged folks like Pumpkin. The frown on her face was full proof that she was all too ready to tangle *and* tussle. If permitted.

I boldly continued despite her look of contempt. "Form a female chorus. Do a skit or dramatic reenactment. Double the cash award for the best pie contest."

"I second that," Miss Dimple, the reigning pie queen, added.

"I don't know..." I shrugged and continued. "Maybe even a parade of floats—"

Flo jumped in before I could finish. "Oh, I like that!" She stood alongside me. "There're more than enough trucks in this town to decorate for a parade. And I'm sure I could get Packer...I mean...*Mr. Sims* to provide a team of award-winning horses to pull a platform decked out with Miss Greenie's roses or to showcase other businesses that would like some such promotion."

"Or..." I continued as if inspired. "What, if not businesses, that platform of roses featured a throne for—"

Tippy was on her feet, finishing in near perfect sync with me. "A float queen?"

Madam Chairperson was hard pressed to control the animated chatter my suggestion created. "Ladies! Please." She continued once silence and order were restored. "Continue, Mrs. Brinks."

I did, proposing that the float queen wasn't about worshiping beauty or placing limitations on us as women. "I'd like to imagine this as an opportunity to honor one of Colemanville's female citizens. Young or old. We can determine the prerequisites or criteria and even establish an application process." My voice softened below its usual register as whatever fire was driving me slowly waned. "If the idea is agreeable, of course. Thank you, Madam Chairperson."

Greenie squeezed my hand as I took my seat. I felt oddly invigorated, fully supported.

Moments later an accepting vote was passed by the showing of raised hands; and the idea was tabled for further discussion until the next meeting.

"So y'all okay with a fake queen floating down the street, but don't want no real dancing?"

I turned in time to see Pumpkin still standing and looking even less unhappy than before as she tossed her pocketbook strap over her arm.

"I'll say! Y'all the ones missing out on finally putting this cow town on the map."

Our eyes met as she sent daggers about the room and her glaring expression slowly faded into something devious. Nearly malicious. Like it might really behoove me to call on Jesus.

She snorted and returned her attention to the room. "Y'all enjoy the rest of y'all's little meeting now. Ya hear?" She tossed me one last glance before exiting, hips sashaying like corn stalks in a hurricane.

"Honey, if looks could kill I'd be mourning my best friend."

I nodded at Greenie's whispered comment and decided that calling on Jesus definitely wasn't a bad idea.

Ten

"What in the blazing bejesus is wrong with Pumpkin Minkins? And it's *choreography*. Not choreographering. But *semi*-burlesque? What in the mismatched socks is that?"

Seated in Miss Dimple's diner, I tried not to laugh at Miss Zayda's looking outdone but failed. My laughter blended with that of the women seated at the table, enjoying servings of Miss Dimple's award-winning peach cobbler and homemade vanilla ice cream.

"Miss Zayda, my mama taught me not to speak ill of my elders so it's best I don't say what I'm thinking."

Dimple snorted delicately. "Flo, honey, you do that if you so choose, but your mama was my best friend so lemme say what Iva would've said if she was here. That skirt might be tight, but Pumpkin ain't wrapped right. Now *that's* an Iva Rae statement."

We were already snickering irreverently when Miss Zayda tapped her temples and added, "Some of her eggs are rolling loose in the kitchen and that gal's about to step on 'em."

"Sis, those loose eggs had that child talking about *Mr.*

Chairman as if Madam Chairperson went and grew something between her legs."

Thanks to Dimple and Zayda we were gone and no good. I felt nearly guilty as our gales of wild merriment whipped about our dining space that was otherwise free of customers.

Colemanville's citizens knew Miss Dimple's establishment shut down early every Friday for our DOLLs meetings. What they weren't privy to was our intimate circle reconvening here afterwards to savor whatever delights Dimple had set aside for the night. We sat at a table in a back alcove not visible from the front windows. It was, as our beloved proprietor liked to say, our private gourmet oasis. Tonight's offering was her blue ribbon-winning peach cobbler with its delectable crust, luscious and tender peaches, and secret blend of spices that left Willard eating two, three helpings whenever we treated ourselves to it.

"Miss Dimple, do you think she should've been allowed to do a burlesque routine?" Tippy asked once we'd re-composed ourselves.

Dimple shook her head. "Honey, you asking the wrong person 'cause risqué ain't my thing. That don't mean some men 'round here wouldn't have been pleased as pudding by Pumpkin's idea."

"That woulda turned this whole town upside down," Greenie added as Dimple sipped her coffee.

She shrugged. "It sho 'nuff woulda. Still...so long as it don't negatively impact me personally...what another woman needs to do to feel free ain't my business. I can't judge her for it."

"What about when the freedom she chooses causes trouble in her romance?"

Our attention turned toward Tippy who sat across from me so focused on Flo that her cousin had to have felt the heat in her gaze.

Heat or simple embarrassment had Flo's cheeks rather pinkish. "Tippy, I swear 'fore heaven you got the biggest mouth in all of creation." She returned her cousin's stare without blinking.

"What? All I did was ask a question."

"You and your canyon mouth ain't never been innocent so stop pretending, *Tipendra*! You being sneaky and tryna tell my business."

"Well, honey hush and let me go from sneaking to speaking, *Floretta*. How 'bout you make Packer understand he ain't your daddy and can't tell you what to do. He can't keep you from finishing college!"

My eyes widened as I looked back and forth between the two who were more sisters than cousins caught up in what seemed to me uncommon hostility.

Flo had her hands on her hips, leaning toward Tippy. "How 'bout you stop acting like some sawdust mannequin who ain't feeling nothing and tell Travis how you really feel about him?"

I flinched as Tippy reared back in her seat as if she'd been slapped. "Sawdust? Just 'cause Travis ain't got *me* hot in the crotch–"

"Alright now, you two, that's enough."

"Miss Dimple, Tippy started it!" Flo cut her eyes at her cousin. "Gotta mouth wide as Texas."

"And you got a wedding in two months so keep your drawers on."

"Guess y'all didn't hear me the first time." Dimple set her coffee cup down delicately as if unfazed by their tension. Her words were evenly spaced, but her tone was nothing to be played with. "I'ma need y'all both to hush this up and listen like you got good sense. See where y'all sitting?" She looked around, her slow gaze prompting us to do the same. "This is my space. When I bought it I bought it fully intending that this diner be a place for friendly fellowship and good food. Not stanky attitudes. So either hush this up and fix whatever's wrong...or excuse yourselves from my premises 'cause these walls ain't built for this."

I watched Flo and Tippy eyeing each other for a long while until, nearly in sync, the cousins exhaled a long breath followed by teary eyes and tender apologies. Zayda, seated between the two, took their hands in hers like the nurturing nurse she was. "Floretta...we can't ever fill Iva's shoes...but if we're needed we're here."

I offered an encouraging smile when Flo looked around the table and our eyes connected.

She half-smiled in return before dumping her woes before the assembled.

I felt for her and how she'd assumed responsibility for her two younger siblings after their mother's death last June only to have that heartbreak compounded when discovering her father was, not only passing, but had a secret, separate life with a white wife over in Jacksonville while Iva Rae was the tainted other woman. Or so she believed. After Doc Everett denied Flo in front of that wife, severely damaging his relationship with his daughter, Flo discovered he'd actually been legally married to Iva. Dimple had been privy to the complicated situation, and it took letters from Iva and Dimple to explain it. After finding peace despite that storm, Flo was in love and engaged to Packer Sims. Now, it seemed as if Packer—a Black Seminole Indian and horse rancher—who'd been supportive of her dreams to return to Oberlin College, was having second thoughts.

Dimple reached across the table and took Flo's hand. "This ain't new news to nobody here, so I ain't gossiping. Flo, Packer's first wife left him for fast living in the big city. That man ain't nothing but scared, honey."

"But I'm not Miss Rudie. I love Packer! I'd never leave him."

"Baby, he's a young man and all he has to go by is the history of his own experiences. Give him time, but stand your ground if you wanna go back to Oberlin. He'll come 'round to it. Now, how's everything coming along for the wedding?"

I listened as Flo brought us up to date, waiting until she'd finished before voicing the idea forming in my head. "Flo, are you doing bridal pictures in your wedding dress?"

She sighed and leaned her head back. "Miss Ilona, I forgot all about that. Seems like things keep falling through the cracks without Mama here."

Her voice broke a bit as she finished.

I pushed my chair back and walked to where she sat. "I'd be honored to paint your wedding portrait if that's agreeable to you."

"Are you serious?" Flo jumped from her chair, suddenly absent of whatever sadness she may have felt. "I'd love that, Miss Ilona! Thank you."

She wrapped her arms about me, hugging me fiercely. I returned the sweet gesture, holding on as her tears wet my dress. "You're absolutely welcome."

"How much would it cost?"

"Nothing. It's my gift to a hardworking young woman raising her brothers and readying herself for marriage even while running her own salon."

She opened her mouth in protest but Greenie cut her off. "I know you ain't too proud to accept a gift, Floretta Eve."

"She's Iva's daughter. She ain't crazy." Zayda's comment had us all laughing in a way that eradicated residual tension and sadness.

Greenie lifted her water glass. "Here's to painted masterpieces by my dearest friend and Colemanville's very own world class artist."

"Amen to that," Miss Dimple chimed in. "And to semi-dressed women everywhere free enough to shake an ass without a care."

Our laughter blended like watercolors with the sound of our clinking glasses as we toasted to liberty in even questionable things.

Eleven

The autumn chill curtailing our customary habit of walking home after gatherings at Miss Dimple's, I rode shotgun, quietly ruminating on the DOLLs meeting as well as our private gathering as Greenie drove. Pumpkin's suggestion might've been outlandish, but I took note of her fearless brashness. That combined with Flo sharing her Packer dilemma with such vulnerability had me feeling open enough to blurt a decision.

"I'm telling Willard and my parents about The Nubian-Kush Collaborative."

"Say what now?" Greenie's truck veered slightly right as if in response to her state of surprise. She corrected Old Faithful, the vehicle that served her well, hauling and delivering the fruits of her harvests in addition to farming implements and necessities. "Did you just say what I think you said?"

"I did." I shivered as the dark night blew frosty breath through my slightly lowered window, whispering a warning that winter wasn't far away and poised to make her arrival with a vengeance. Or perhaps it was the prospect of facing unnecessary opposition that left me chilled.

I rolled up the window and glanced at Greenie's profile from my place on the passenger side.

"I don't feel like falsifying anything. I want to be proud of what I create, whether or not Willard, Mother, or Father support me. I'm tired of feeling like I'm hiding or overlooked...and always apologizing."

"LoLo, honey I hear you. And good for you!" Greenie whistled low and slow. "Only God knows how they'll react, but you have my support however it's needed."

I exchanged a smile with Greenie before turning toward the window. I blew against it, doodling in the foggy condensation it created as we rode home in companionable silence.

Greenie's Old Faithful didn't have a radio like Father's Pontiac, but after all of the hubbub and interactions of the night I didn't mind the quiet. By the time we pulled up in front of my house I felt mellow yet determined.

"Tell Mother Robertson my persimmons are looking real good this season. She's gonna have a field day baking all her persimmon breads and cookies. And remember I'm in your corner, friend..."

We pressed palms and finished our age-old vow together, "Through thick and thin."

I exited Old Faithful, smiling and appreciative.

I waved as Greenie pulled off and headed up the walkway, tightening my coat about me against the cool breeze, fortifying my resolve with repeated, internal speech.

I am honest. I am decisive. I will speak openly no matter their opinions.

I paused, startled by the sound of soft banging only to recognize it as the door of the outhouse out back being knocked about by the wind. I inhaled expecting to be hit by odorous smells but remembered the latrine had been removed, its cavern filled with lime and sawdust to prevent such unpleasantness.

Sawdust from Gabriel's furniture store and his handiwork.

I refused thoughts of Gabe and his masterful craftsmanship and rushed up the walkway and into the house where lamplight from the parlor welcomed me in. The house was otherwise dark. Quiet.

I glanced at my wristwatch and saw that it was after ten, far later than I usually returned after our Friday night DOLLs meetings. Clearly, we'd stayed at Dimple's eating peach cobbler and chatting longer than I'd realized. I hung my coat in the hall closet and headed toward my parents' bedroom hoping they were still awake so I could speak with them and Willard.

My heart beat kicked up a bit as I saw light flowing out from beneath their door.

I knocked and waited, knocking again when there was no answer. Quietly, I eased the door open and found my parents fast asleep; Mother's Bible resting on her lap. I moved the Bible onto the bedside table and turned off the lamp before exiting as quietly as I'd entered.

There's still Willard...

No light spilled from underneath our bedroom door. Instead, the hallway reverberated with the hearty sounds of Willard's snores.

I exhaled, disappointed that my bold revelation would have to hold until morning, and headed for the bathroom for my nighttime routine of face-washing and brushing my teeth. Despite disappointment, I hummed softly while imagining myself in front of that arts committee in Raleigh.

You can do whatever you put your mind to, Sweet Rivers.

My humming ended as Gabe's deep voice swirled about the private space. I stared at my mirrored reflection, telling myself how inappropriate it was to be hearing the opinion of a lost love. I brushed aside notions of Gabe's belief in me and reached for the jar of Flo's proprietary cold cream only to find it missing from its place on the shelf.

Puzzled, I searched for it unsuccessfully.

"Willard must've accidentally knocked it into the wastebasket again."

I looked, but didn't find it there, instead finding Willard's washcloth where it had fallen on the floor between the laundry basket and the trash bin. I picked it up, ready to drop it in the basket where it belonged. My fingers encountered a thick white substance similar to yet different from my cold cream. I studied the unfamiliar wad before sniffing it gingerly.

The odor was metallic, yet oddly human, and nothing like the sweet calming fragrance of Flo's product. It was off putting and I tossed the towel in the laundry to get rid of its unpleasantness before washing my hands. Moments later I was down on my hands and knees, searching underneath the sink for my missing cold cream without producing anything.

"Use whatever's available until you can get a replacement jar come morning."

I followed my own advice, disliking wastefulness. And my options.

Petroleum jelly. Hair pomade. Willard's aftershave lotion. I reached for the petroleum jelly at the rear of the cabinet, accidentally knocking over my husband's secret stash of Wild Turkey hidden at the back. Liquor spewed all over the place thanks to the cap not being screwed on correctly.

"Dear, Lord, today..."

I righted the bottle and placed it on the floor before racing to the linen closet. Grabbing a towel, I hurried back, eager to clean the mess before anything was irreparably damaged.

Nauseated by the smell of liquor permeating the small space, I quickly removed items from beneath the sink and used the towel to mop up the mess only to feel a slight give in the cabinet floor slats beneath my hand.

I paused my cleaning and pressed again.

A board shifted. I wiggled it bit by bit, eventually removing it only to realize a small space existed beneath the board, leaving a gap between the cabinet bottom and the subfloor. I might have shrugged it off without further interest except something lay in the cramped space underneath and was only slightly visible. I placed the board aside when finding a newspaper folded in half and tucked in that space underneath the bathroom sink.

"Why in the world is a copy of *The Colemanville Chronicle* down here?"

It rained down its contents nestled safely inside as I removed it and it accidentally fell open.

Postcards gushed out, sliding across the floor with abandon like birds on broken wings. One strayed from the pack, landing on my lap. I stared down at the postcard and those about the bathroom floor, my mouth slowly opening.

They were plastered with old photos. Sepia-toned. And flagrant.

I stared in disbelief at the one on my lap, unable to touch it.

I was an artist. I loved the human form, was mesmerized by its lines, curves, and intricacies. But these scattered postcards were more than mere art. They bore sepia photographs of naked women in decadent positions. Varying complexions. Varying physiques. Their poses ranged from coyly seductive to brazenly scandalous and severely wanton. It was far from art. It was exploitative, fulfilling the lewd appetite of my husband.

Their flagrant exposure left me speechless.

Questions flooded my mind. Inertia arrested my limbs. I felt hollow. Cold. Confused. I grabbed the newspaper, as if it was to blame, and checked its publication date.

It was two years ago, May. And on our first wedding anniversary.

"Dear. God. Willard...why?"

I reasoned with myself that the date of the newspaper wasn't proof of the longevity of his indulgence. Yet, I knew my husband. He was frugal and would have put that paper to use the same day of its publication. He didn't hold onto periodicals after reading them and he was never wasteful.

Doesn't matter if it was two years ago or yesterday. He's been doing sordid things.

I told myself not to be judgmental or unfair.

"These postcards aren't proof of anything other than his misguided need for looking. They don't necessarily indicate further wrongdoing..."

You just put a soiled washcloth in the hamper.

I stared at the dirty laundry container that seemed to mock me as it sat there holding the evidence of Willard's recent engagement with these decadent women frozen in time and impossible poses for his selfish fulfillment.

The substance on that washcloth that wasn't cold cream testified that he'd, that night, spent time actively engaged with them.

My eyes drifted shut as bitter truth hit me over the head, as I relived Willard's constant condescension and lack of affection. His abandoning relations with me midway every Tuesday and Thursday and sequestering himself in the restroom only to return after long gaps of time. Terse. Shifty-eyed.

Yes, I suspected he sequestered in the bathroom to bring himself to completion. Still, I'd never imagined that being with the aid of lewd postcards of naked women.

I buried my face in my hands and breathed ragged breaths that couldn't minimize the truth. I was married to a man who preferred the company and bodies of inanimate women to my living flesh.

. . .

The small lantern offered little light. Shadows wavered along my path as I stepped deeper into the night, heading for my art shed. The sound of the outhouse door being blown back and forth by the wind accompanied me as the brisk breath of night stroked my neck. Somewhere in the distance an owl hooted, its mournful notes melding with my loneliness.

The lantern light seemingly expanded as I secured the door behind me after entering my sacred domain. Here the shadows were soft and welcoming. I accepted their elongated, misshapen embrace and moments later had my materials laid out and waiting. With a clean sheet affixed to my easel I sat, brush in hand, watercolors ready to purge myself of bitter hues.

I dipped my brush in the paint and stroked it against the canvas without real intention, feeling tainted. Used.

I'd endured Willard's blame and accusations on far too many occasions. His list of my shortcomings felt extensive. My not earning enough that created our inability to afford our own house. My not conceiving during our twice-weekly incomplete acts of intimacy. His constant critiques of how I dressed. His dismissiveness of my artistic talent and passion. His repeated warning that my hips were spreading. In too many ways Willard had done his damnedest to make me feel like a failure and burden when all along he was the insufficient partner not fully present in this marriage.

"I'm not the defective, detached one. He is!"

Sudden fury flowed through me, projecting heat down my arm and into my painting. My practice of approaching my every creative work with quiet reverence flew out the window leaving a jagged wildness in its place.

Slashing colors across that canvas so carelessly felt sacrilegious. Liberating. Neatness was ignored. Watercolors splattered everywhere until fury exhausted herself and I felt empty, open.

I don't love my husband.

That admission slowly seeped out of me as I stared at the caricature of Willard I'd just painted. It was buffoonish and exaggerated. Yet, oddly accurate. Shameful or not, I relished its irreverence.

"I hold no hate for my husband...but I hold no love either."

I'd been soft spoken my entire life. That didn't make me ignorant of the power of my voice.

My voice held and hinted at a much needed shift. Speaking those facts aloud brought me back to the center of myself somehow. It didn't feel good admitting I lacked deep, let alone heartfelt, affection for the man I'd married. Neither was that admission a knee-jerk response to his solitary activities, his pornographic pleasures.

I wasn't overreacting. Truth was true. I'd never loved Willard, and didn't think I ever would.

Marrying him had been an act of contrition. And resignation. My first love was gone, a living casualty of the war who, after being injured, chose to fade into the wide world beyond. My decision to wait for his return reduced my mother to weeping as if the world would end and sent Father into a state of severe outrage that resulted in a stroke that nearly ended his existence.

Guilt stemming from my part in my father's near-death experience was what deflated my resistance. It left me compliant, obedient. My acceptance of Willard as Father's choice for my preferred mate was penance and my gift to his recovery. I'd swallowed my wants and wishes and chose to make the best of it, desperately praying I'd grow to love him. Willard seemed to have a decided interest in me, but it was one-sided and, clearly, held an ulterior motive. Or was disingenuous at best. For me romantic sparks and attraction weren't present. Still, I stoically walked away from notions of passion and relied on his humanity, his decency. He was educated, ambitious, and had big dreams. I knew him from college and relied on that familiarity. I had faith for a comfortable existence and daily prayed we'd grow into a reasonable state of affection. I pushed aside misgivings and after a brief two-month courtship Willard and I were married.

I studied my unflattering painting of his likeness before snatching it from the easel and slowly making confetti of it.

Like snowflakes, the shredded pieces floated to the floor. I didn't mind the mess, or the lone tear sauntering slowly down my cheek. I didn't mourn the loss of nonexistent affection or the sad state of affairs my marriage was in. Both felt inconsequential compared to an inescapable truth suddenly slamming through my chest.

I closed my eyes and spoke it aloud as if doing so could lessen its impact.

"I never stopped loving Gabriel Thurman."

Twelve

The sun played a peek-a-boo game high above Colemanville, sliding and hiding behind cotton candy clouds before reappearing again. Softened by the season, the sun's rays sprinkled golden motes down from heaven that danced carefree in the cool morning air. Those sunbeams were like tiny guiding lights in the early quiet of Saturday gently surrounding me as I headed toward Grayson's, my supply kit in hand.

I wish I could paint this in its entirety.

The autumnal colors of fall had exploded all over Colemanville and the artist in me wanted to plop down in the middle of the road and capture every shade and nuance of its beauty. Gold, crimson, and pumpkin colored leaves undulated in the breeze, some detaching themselves from proud tree limbs to playfully swirl about my feet. Fall blooming perennials added their glory to the day with the pale pink of Baby Joe pye weed, the purple of star-shaped asters and bush sage that was a favorite of hummingbirds.

I paused in hopes of a hummingbird sighting that didn't

occur, only to find clusters of orange and red ladybugs on a rock alongside the road as I moved on.

"Ladybugs are a symbol of good fortune and hope."

It didn't matter whether or not I believed that myth. I was in no position to refuse it. If fortune would turn in my favor and destroy what felt like weights constricting my neck, I'd welcome its fortuitous freedom.

Having laid in bed last night studying the dark ceiling and contemplating life for hours on end, I was no longer stunned speechless by Willard's stash of nude postcards. Initial shock had given way to a dull, bitter ache that wanted to make itself at home in the middle of my chest. I'd prayed, cried, and otherwise resisted tender pain while repeatedly telling myself I wasn't inferior. Despite my husband's outside interests, I *was* a complete woman.

I wasn't to blame.

Such pictures wouldn't exist if men's depraved appetites didn't demand them.

I found Willard's appetite for nude and lewd pornographic images highly baffling in light of what I considered to be his rigid, purist tendencies. His insistence that the lights remain off as well as his preference for silence and my non-participation during our marital acts had led me to believe he was disinterested in intimate activities and that what we engaged in was sheer obligation. Duty not passion. Pre-scheduled. Twice-weekly. Were these factors and behaviors not clear indications of my husband's repressed nature and his absence of a robust carnal need?

Apparently, Willard had secret needs that I could never satiate.

I inhaled a deep breath, raised my head, and slowly released it into cool autumn air scented with pine and jasmine and attempted to solace myself with the fact that Willard had not stepped beyond the bonds of our marriage. At least not literally. Still, his selfish preference for private time with his lusty paper doll women stung like a betrayal.

"But you don't even love him."

Last night I made that unfortunate admission. Doing so didn't make me cruel or unfeeling. It made me honest. I was a living being with feelings. Despite a lack of love in marriage I'd been kind, compassionate, supportive, and faithful. Now, I experienced a new longing to have that reciprocated even while sensing that Willard might feel the same way about me that I felt about him: loveless.

I kicked a pebble from my path and watched it roll away.

"Lord, what kind of mess have we made?"

My heart sank a bit beneath the weight of my reflections. Not only was my marriage lacking beautiful and endearing attributes and qualities, but a specter of inadequacy stepped from the shadows where it had been impatiently waiting. It whispered horribly of my inability to please my husband. According to its whispered hiss, I was deficient in my womanhood as well as sensuality.

"I will not be reduced by Willard Brinks' lack of affection or nonexistent desire for me."

I crossed the footbridge that linked Colemanville's residential district to downtown, countering horrid lies out loud.

My husband's habits had left me without proof that I could please him. Still, I couldn't let his deceitfulness discolor me as inadequate.

Baby, some folks're fool enough to mistake your quietness for weakness. Shame on 'em.

I paused mid stride as my grandmother's voice came to me, floating on the wind.

M'Dear passed away when I was nineteen. There on that footbridge I craved her presence. I longed to embrace her again, to lean on her wisdom. I'd inherited her demeanor. She was quiet. Gracious. Yet, unmistakably dynamic without being authoritative.

I called her softly as if she could hear me from her place in eternity.

"M'Dear, what does my quiet personality have to do with Willard's actions?"

I waited, not seeing a correlation, but fully expecting an answer. The wind responded with a gentle kiss against my face, but the heart of M'Dear was silent.

I pushed forward on my journey, my mind tumbling with questions.

Had it been easy for a person as outspoken and demanding as Willard to misinterpret my soft-spokenness for weakness? Did he think I was inherently prone to accept disrespect when I'd simply embraced being my authentic self? That authentic self honored others and preferred kindness to crudeness and cruelty. That didn't give him license to mistreat me or our marriage.

"This whole thing feels crude and rude."

I increased my pace, trying to outdistance those feelings the same as I had earlier that morning as I'd quickly, quietly bathed and dressed while the rest of my family slept—unwilling to continue being treated as a disregarded daughter, wife, or woman. I'd phoned Miz Grayson before hurrying to my art shed and collecting my tools while telling myself I no longer wanted to live a quiet life.

Being heard and seen is a basic right.

"Hey, now, Ilona! Good morning."

Miz Grayson stood outside the mercantile, apron about her waist, broom in hand.

I returned her wave as well as her greeting, admiring her fortitude and ability to continue their business despite her husband's losing his sight as a result of having the sugar. Or diabetes. Mr. Grayson was no longer the one behind the counter cheerfully greeting customers. Still, he faithfully accompanied his wife to their place of business on a regular basis. He was able to assist in small tasks despite his sightlessness, but for the majority of the day he sat on a chair in the corner of the store keeping his wife company. They'd hired Tippy part-time to help manage otherwise.

"Thank you for taking my call so early this morning."

"Honey, me and Mr. Grayson gets up with the roosters so you didn't disturb our sleep one bit. I'm just tickled pink you're finally fitting us in." She resumed her sweeping. "I saw how you prettied up Iva Rae's front window..." She glanced across the street at Iva's House of Beauty. "I suppose I should refer to it as Flo's now seeing as how Iva's gone." She paused her task. "Lord, that was a sweet woman. Rest her soul. Still takes some getting used to." She shook her head and looked at me. "Change ain't easy for someone my age."

As long as I'd known Miz Grayson she'd been a gregarious talker who could stitch together a stream of sentences on one breath. Right then was no exception.

I patiently listened as she segued from Flo's new ownership, and the library built last fall, to the town's harvest festival Monday as if all were interconnected.

"Lord, lemme quit jabbering and let you get about your painting. I got things inside the store I'd best tend to. You need anything?"

I patted my kit and assured her I didn't.

"Well, I can at least bring you a chair or crate or something to set that on. Gimme a minute."

She returned momentarily, setting a crate on the wooden walkway for my use.

"Thank you."

"Honey, don't thank me! Just make my storefront window prettier than Iva's...I mean, Flo's."

We laughed, but I knew she was serious.

Downtown Colemanville's merchants were famous for engaging in friendly rivalry. Each claimed to have the cleanest, prettiest, or best laid establishment. Windows sparkled in the dappled morning light and walkways were spotless as the front facades of their businesses reflected pride of ownership.

"I'll do my best."

"I know so well." She patted my shoulder and returned indoors, leaving me to my craft.

I'ma paint this window sign like I'm Aaron Douglas or Rembrandt.

I poked my head in the store to greet Mr. Grayson before removing my sweater, exposing my smock underneath, and placing the outerwear Mother had knitted atop the crate Miz Grayson had provided despite the morning chill. I rubbed my hands to warm them, knowing that in a matter of minutes the cool temperatures would be nonexistent. Immersing in art, no matter its form, released an internal energy that fueled me, often leaving me unmindful of the external world—its cold, its heat. Art took me away. Art spoke for me.

Grayson's Mercantile.

I sketched bold letters across the window with a wax stick in a design that proved decorative and borderline elaborate. The proprietor had given me carte blanche to create as I pleased, and knowing Miz Grayson, the more distinctive, the more her signage stood out and grabbed attention the better.

Frame it to make it more prominent.

I adhered to my idea and carefully drew a circular border about the text, letting the store's name float through it. I stepped from the walkway onto the road in order to inspect my work when finished.

"I don't like that G." Using the cloth rag in my kit, I carefully erased the wax letter and recreated it until satisfied. "*Voila*! That's it."

I set about gathering my brushes and gold gilt paint when pleased with the outcome.

"I am ready for this masterpiece."

I grinned at my over exaggeration of my task before closing my eyes and softly inviting my muse to join me. I never approached a project without her. I welcomed and needed the spirit of creativity in all things large or small, simple or complex. Even signage painting.

It's beneath you. It lacks dignity.

I ignored Willard's voice suddenly booming in the back of my mind. He was a contradiction, claiming such work was beneath me even while denigrating my gift on one hand and demanding I forge masterful work with his next breath.

I pushed his unsolicited opinion and negativity aside. "I'm painting for myself. Not him."

And Lord pardon me but I'm not forging a damn thing.

My chin lifted with determination as my brush met paint and I gave myself to the joy at hand. The flow of my gift was immediate. Her treasured embrace wrapped me securely and we moved as one as my brush floated across that plate glass window with sweeping strokes and tight curves that brought vision to reality.

I stepped back for a better perspective.

The letters were beautifully painted, rather like calligraphy. Still, it seemed as if something was missing.

"Outline the right side of each gold letter in white. That'll give dimension and a bit of flourish."

I finished moments later and reexamined my work. It brought a calm sense of satisfaction to me. I dropped my brushes in the large mason jar of cleaning liquid I kept for that purpose and smiled. I was pleased.

"Oooh, that's some kind of pretty!"

I whirled to face the woman who'd appeared behind me without detection. She stood where the road met the walkway, admiring the newly painted window. She looked so like her son that it was practically eerie. They shared the same honey colored eyes, strong jaw, and silky brown skin. Her beauty had made him heart-stopping handsome. "Good morning, Miz Thurman!"

"Morning, baby. When you finish wasting your time tryna doll up this broken down Cracker Jack box Georgia Grayson got the nerve to call a store, come on across the street and put your skills to good use on a *real* business."

"Tilda Thurman, if you don't take your crossed-eyed, crooked-knee having self on away from here!" The proprietor of Grayson's Mercantile appeared in the doorway as if magically drawn by the scent of a competitor.

"I'll take crossed eyes and crooked knees to your flat, web-toed platypus feet any day of God's good week, Georgia Grayson. Now, gon' back inside your little pretend store and stay outta grown folks' business. And while you're at it, check on your blind husband. He might need something."

"Tilda, had your man lost his vision y'all might still be together, heifer."

I stood amazed by the unsavory comments being volleyed back and forth between the two women until they'd exhausted their strong opinions.

"I gotta get *my real* enterprise ready for business and ain't about to spend no more energy with your catawampus misconceptions. Bye, Georgia Grayson."

"Bye, Tilda Thurman."

They turned to go their separate ways only for Miz Grayson to suddenly remember something.

"Oh, girl, wait! There's a couple slices of that Sock It To Me cake left from yesterday. You coming back around lunch time to have some with me?"

"You ain't gotta ask me twice. See you then."

I stood, mouth half open, thinking if an outsider had been privy to what I'd just witnessed they'd never believe Miz Thurman and Miz Grayson were lifelong best friends.

Miz Thurman waited for Miz Grayson to go indoors before approaching me. "I'm serious now, Ilona. If ain't nothing else holding your attention after you finish here come on over to the furniture store and pick yourself up some more business. I love supporting enterprising young Colored women."

I turned toward the establishment at the opposite end of Fig Street, contemplating how best to decline the offer but Miz Thurman hurried on as if intuiting my intent.

"Much as I wish you two woulda stayed together there ain't no need for worrying. You ain't gonna encounter Gator. He don't start work 'til late on Saturdays. Fast as you paint you'll be finished before he even knows you been there."

I nodded at Gabe's mother, appreciating her shrewd perception.

My path hadn't crossed with Gabe's since that black cat ran in the road deciding my bike and I needed to be airborne. Mere days had passed, yet it felt like an impossible eternity since he'd lifted, aided, kissed me.

My face felt flush with the truth that I was the one doing the kissing. Gabe had simply stood there, a solid mass of disinterest.

"Yes, ma'am. I'll be there shortly. Soon as I finish outlining these letters." The extra money would come in handy and keep me from having to make a withdrawal from the box of feminine hygiene products that served as my bank to help supplement my travel expenses to Raleigh next weekend. I planned to paint like the wind and be gone before Gabe showed his face. God forbid he should arrive before I finished, but if he did there was no need to worry about the appearance of impropriety with others present. Nor was there a fear of anything inappropriate occurring between us.

I'm married. And it's crystal clear Gabe no longer holds any affection for me.

I squared my shoulders and resumed my work on the Graysons' window and swallowed that hardcore truth as well as the notion that I should focus on healing my relationship with Willard. Regardless if my marriage improved or remained the same, the love Gabe and I once shared was stagnant water under the proverbial bridge.

Thirteen

The Graysons' signage came out so nicely! I wish I had my old camera so I could take a picture.

Mother had confiscated my camera before I finished high school and I hadn't seen it since.

I stood huddled up with Miz Grayson and Tippy, taking my time admiring my work and committing the freshly painted design to memory. It seemed to glow and preen in the autumn light like somebody's primadonna of signs.

Miz Grayson's satisfaction was even more radiant. "Honey, I'm having this printed on everything possible from our bags to our shopkeeper aprons. Ilona, you outdid yourself. It's marvelous!" She clapped her hands. "Don't you think so, Tippy?"

"I definitely do! It gives the place new character."

"Indeed it does. Soon as it dries I'ma bring Grayson out here and describe it to him so his mind can see it."

"You need to let Floretta touch that head and give it some deliverance. Walking 'round here looking like somebody's electrocuted rabbit."

We looked behind us to find Miz Thurman standing in

front of her furniture store down the street, hands on her hips and looking like she meant business.

"Tilda, ain't nobody studying you. You just jealous 'cause your crooked little storefront is suffering from a lack of class."

"You wanna know what you ain't suffering from, Georgia? A lack of ass!"

Miz Grayson sucked her teeth dismissively. "Oooh, come on here, Tippy. Get me in my mercantile before I walk across this road and slap Tilda more ignorant than she already is."

"I heard that!"

"You should seeing as how your ears're big as my—"

"Miz Grayson, tomorrow's the sabbath." Tippy's caution curtailed her boss's repartee.

"Thank you, Tippy. Ol' hag best be glad I don't believe in cussing so close to Sunday."

Tippy and I exchanged an amused look as the two headed indoors.

"Don't forget to save me some cake!"

Miz Grayson poked her head outside to answer her friend. "You got it, honey. I'm going in here right now to dust it with powdered sugar and a little touch of arsenic."

Tilda Thurman laughed heartily. "Come on here, Ilona baby, and get my window looking better than that witch's."

I gathered my sweater and kit and stepped onto Fig Street, Downtown Colemanville's main thoroughfare. The hustle and bustle of Saturday shopping and activity hadn't begun yet. The street remained calm, quiet.

Enjoy it while you can.

There was something soothing in the gentleness of morning. Soon enough there'd be patrons in and out of the mercantile, the newly built library at the end of the street, or Flo's salon and Mr. Wilcox's barbershop and shoe shine, getting themselves right and ready for Sunday service the next day. Dimple's diner on the edge of town near Copper Lake was the regular spot for downhome cooking and plenty of fellowship, but the burger shack and ice cream stand located here in the hub of town provided refreshment as well. The drug store included space for Dr. Mercer's clinic, but we had no movie theater or filling station and had to drive to Jacksonville for either amenity.

Greenie and I sometimes treated ourselves to a movie there, but the enjoyment was too often marred by having to enter via the rear staircase to sit in the small, segregated Coloreds only balcony that was typically overcrowded and rarely, if ever, cleaned. Add to that indignity being served last, even when we arrived first, at the malt shop or the inability to dine there and being made to pick our orders up at the rear window. Or having to pump our own petrol despite Jacksonville having a full-service filling station because racism wouldn't dare allow the white attendants to serve us.

Thank God there's talk of getting our own station annexed onto Harvey's Automotive.

I took in my surroundings while crossing Fig Street and felt immense gratitude and pride. Compared to major cities, Colemanville was tiny. Quaint. Ours was a town founded and built by and for Colored folks, a safe place where neighbors weren't strangers but family and friends. To the wide world beyond, Colemanville might not seem like much. Still, I was thankful to be the product of a place that felt like a hidden gem.

My gratitude includes the money I just made and tucked in my brassiere.

I unconsciously patted the pin money Miz Grayson had paid that was now safely deposited in my Bank of the Breasts as M'Dear jokingly referred to the tiny satin pouch she kept tucked against her bosom. I remembered my grandfather as being intrinsically kind, but a bit on the stingy side. Life with him had formed M'Dear's belief that a woman should have something of her own and keep a little for herself versus being fully dependent on a husband.

I guess M'Dear and I had more in common than I realized.

I mounted the walkway where Miz Thurman waited, embarrassment flushing my skin as I considered how I trusted Willard with the bulk of my earnings from teaching art at the school and his doling out an allowance in return. That was a practice I was unwilling to continue. Going forward, whatever I earned I would keep and determine how it was saved. Or spent.

"Whatcha need, baby?"

"Nothing, Miz Thurman, except I'd like to empty this mason jar and refill it with fresh water." I preferred my brush cleaning liquid, but I hadn't anticipated multiple painting jobs that morning and the fluid in the jar was already murky from painting at the mercantile. Water would suffice for now.

"Come on in and help yourself to the storeroom sink. I'ma sit right here in front this window and conjure up a design that'll make Georgia stinking green with envy."

I laughed as she sat in a wide, solid-looking rocking chair and set it in motion. "That's a beautiful chair."

She passed a hand over its curved, intricately carved arms and rocked gently. "It is, ain't it? Gator made it."

I shimmied away from the warmth that hit my belly at the mention of her son's name. "Miz Thurman...you mind me asking how you and Miz Grayson are best friends...when you...?"

She completed my unfinished question. "When we go at it like Tasmanian devils trapped in a sack?" She laughed. "Honey, we just putting on. Clowning and playing the dozens like we did when we was kids. But lemme tell you this." She leaned back as if demonstrating the chair's strength. "I'll get a gun from Gator's rifle collection, shoot first, and ask not one question if anybody *ever* tried to hurt that woman. And I bet you'd do the same for Clementine."

I smiled at her use of Greenie's birth name. "I hope I never have to aim a rifle at anyone for any reason...but for a loved one...I suppose I would if the situation called for it."

She nodded emphatically. "Every woman deserves that kind of loyalty. Now, go'n back and get your brushes and stuff ready. And help yourself to anything you need."

"Yes, ma'am." I headed for the room at the rear of the store, admiring various pieces of furniture as I went. Each had a look of solidity and fine craftsmanship. Wood gleamed. Designs were exquisite. Beds. Nightstands. Side tables. Dining tables. Chairs. Chests and curio cabinets. They were built to last and reflected pride of workmanship.

They're beautiful works of art in their own right.

I entered the storeroom, mind on the loveliness I'd just seen while heading for the small restroom intent on using its sink. Vaguely conscious of the smells of varnish, wood polish, and other craft-related solvents, I pushed the door open only to freeze at the sight of God's goodness.

I should've turned around and scuttled out of there fast as Willard could finish a slice of German chocolate cake and request a second. I didn't. I stood motionless, mouth open as I admired the pure art of Gabriel Thurman standing before a small wall mounted mirror, razor in hand, shaving cream partially covering his jaw and absolutely shirtless.

"Ilona?" He turned toward me, razor frozen in air, expression reflecting that he was as shocked by my unexpected appearance as I was by his state of undress.

Delicious shock moored me in place as I slowly considered his magnificence.

Broad shoulders tapered into a lean waist. A well-proportioned upper body boasted masculine strength. His physique was muscular. Defined. Immaculate. I wanted to touch the warm chestnut skin, to experience its velvet.

My gaze made a slow journey to his face. I barely registered Gabe hurriedly wiping away shaving cream. My eyes were too busy sauntering over his physique.

I'd loved him in our younger years when our courtship was disapproved of by my parents and so heavily chaperoned that holding hands was a decadent rebellion. Despite my parents' restrictions and the intrusive protection of my older sisters, we'd managed to steal time alone on occasion. Back then, in those innocent moments, the demonstration of our love and affection had been limited to sweet kisses and tender, stimulating touches that we managed to terminate before they went too far. We'd never experienced intimacy or oneness with each other. Standing in his presence I suddenly wanted to saturate my senses with all that made Gabriel who he was, and to taste and kiss everything I'd ever missed. Now and then.

The idea of indulging that kind of fantasy sent heat through my starved nerve endings and left me reaching out to him in an attempt to satisfy myself. Even if only through touch.

His body tensed then relaxed as I touched his face. His shoulders. His chest. He was sculpture and flesh. Mortal. Yet perfection.

Lord, if those britches slip an inch I'm finished.

I needed to shield my eyes from the sight of his Levi's riding so indecently low on his hips, but I didn't.

"I ain't sure why you're back here, but you shouldn't be!" The gruffness in his tone yanked my attention from his lower region. But it didn't stop me from continuing my exploration. I dared to touch the hard, flatness of his belly. His was a rock compared to Willard's.

His entire being is beyond comparison.

That truth brought a smile to my lips as I touched his left

arm, admired its strength even while turning my attention to what remained of his right appendage.

A tattoo of a panther's head, its mouth open and snarling, decorated the upper remains, with words tattooed underneath it: Come Out Fighting.

I stared fascinated, not repulsed, by the taut skin and intricate scars covering the stump of his elbow where his arm no longer existed. It was a tapestry, a canvas depicting what he'd experienced fighting for a country that refused to see him as human. A tender pang shot through my chest. I reached out to touch his arm with affection.

As if a reflex, Gabe instantly stepped back. His response pulled me from whatever fascination I may have felt and hurled me into fresh memories of Willard's rejection. This man who my heart still craved detested my touch, needing it about as much as my husband.

"I apologize. I didn't mean to be intrusive." I whirled toward the bathroom door, intent on leaving before the sudden tears filling my eyes could embarrass me.

I flinched at Gabe's reaching over my head and shutting the door before I could exit.

"Ilona..." His earlier gruffness was replaced by tenderness. He turned me toward him and his touch was sweeter than I remembered. "Why're you here?"

I held my paint kit aloft as if it was a complete explanation. He barely glanced at it before taking it from me and placing it on the floor near my feet.

My heart skipped wildly as he moved closer, his gaze never leaving mine, until we stood toe to toe, body to body. I wanted to feel something other than the overwhelming heat and hunger his nearness evoked but my whole self seemed centered on all the things I shouldn't crave and couldn't possibly do. Still, I stayed. I let him touch my chin and lift my face toward his. And when his lips hesitated mere inches above mine, I stood on the tips of my toes and completed the connection that proved sublime.

Don't tell anyone, but I kissed Gabe Thurman.

I instantly remembered sitting in church and whispering that truth in Greenie's ear the day after Gabe and I first kissed. Kissing him so many years later I experienced the same secretive deliciousness.

Somewhere in the back of my mind, my morals loudly screamed that I should not be doing this. I was married and this was illicit. That didn't prevent me from sinking deeper into his embrace or wanting to wordlessly convey to Gabe my realization of how much I absolutely loved and missed him.

You've got your lips on a man you're not married to...in a bathroom?!

Another time and place that would have shamed me into behaving properly, left me embarrassed at conducting myself this way particularly in such surroundings. But thoughts of Willard's salacious activities in the privacy of our restroom flashed through my mind and filled me with uncommon defiance.

Still, my soul was certain. This wasn't a tit for tat revenge. This was my heart opening a door that led back to where I belonged.

This was sweet as watercolors on a spring day. This was homecoming.

Fourteen

"Ilona, baby, you finding everything you need back there?"

Gabe and I released each other quickly, albeit reluctantly. He steadied me as I stumbled from the sudden loss of his anchoring embrace, as well as the sensation of being ripped from the sweetest kiss I'd ever experienced.

"Oh, Jesus! Your mother cannot find us like this." I panicked at the sound of Miz Thurman's approach. My shaking hands left me struggling with the door knob in an attempt to escape our tight confines. I couldn't afford to be caught in a compromising position, neither was I willing to subject Gabe to scrutiny or judgment. I needed to get out front where I should have been before I kissed my first love and lost my God given good sense.

"Hey. Sweet Rivers. Take a breath." Gabe's customary calm cut through my anxiousness.

I inhaled and exhaled slowly, wondering how he could be so unflustered. I tried not to but couldn't help admiring his form as he snatched an undershirt hanging from a wall hook and slipped it on. His movements were swift and efficient belying his being an amputee.

"Stay here."

He eased from the room, closing the door behind him before I could protest. I leaned against it and bowed my head, wishing away this predicament. Had I gone straight home after finishing at the Graysons', this never would have happened. It was enough to make me wonder if I'd accepted Miz Thurman's offer subconsciously hoping to encounter Gabe. Even if I had, the possibility of us kissing hadn't factored into that consideration.

"*Gator*? Son, whatchu doing here so early?"

"Hey, Ma. It was half past two when I finished up that grandfather clock for Mr. Withers so I bunked here last night. I was too tired to drive."

My heart raced like one of Packer's prized stallions as I listened to their voices on the opposite side of the door.

"That explains why I didn't see your big boat feet parked under my breakfast table this morning."

Gabe's laughter was a warm wave of joy that felt like sunshine to me. "Come on, Ma. You know I get lost in wood once I start working."

"Yes, son, you do. Well, how'd it turn out? I must've been too busy fussing with Georgia to notice it."

"It's a nice piece if I say so myself. Let me show it to you—"

"Wait now. Where'd Ilona get to?"

"I suppose the restroom."

"You *suppose*? Is she or ain't she? I know you paid attention! And why ain't you dressed yet? Saturday's a nice shopping day and I need you ready when folks roll in."

"I'm a master craftsman. Not a salesperson."

"Boy, you gonna add unemployed to your list if you ain't ready when the store opens."

Their laughter blended harmoniously.

Busy eavesdropping, I jumped like grease in a skillet at the sound of Miz Thurman knocking.

"Ilona, you alright in there?"

"Yes, ma'am, I am."

"I'm going up front with Gator so he can show off this new grandfather clock of his. Join us when you finish your business."

I assured her I would, and felt ten degrees of guilty as their voices faded in the distance.

Kissing Gabe was like rainbows after a tempestuous storm. It watered my dry places that were cracked and fissured, but it also made me unfaithful. That weighty truth felt even heavier knowing I'd misused Miz Thurman's graciousness. She'd invited me here in support of my craft, not to play the harlot on her premises.

Miz Thurman possessed a healthy dose of common sense as well as motherly intuition. One look at me and she'd know firsthand something was far from right. That is if she hadn't already detected as much from her son. I was tempted to slip out the back way, but knew that would only complicate the situation and I'd have to explain myself eventually. Despite the temptation, I didn't run. I told myself to stay where I was and face whatever music I'd orchestrated.

I am capable. I am strong. I will not lie. I will not run.

M'Dear had taught me to speak life to myself despite any challenges. I did so while taking my time to breathe deeply and gather my wits while considering the tiny bathroom space about me.

Clothing hung from hooks. Men's toiletries lined a shelf. Instinctively I determined that they were Gabe's. And despite his explanation of sleeping at the store to complete a project, something in me wondered if his family's store had become home for him.

"Ilona, mind your business."

I flushed the contents of my mason jar down the commode before refilling it at the sink while assessing myself in the small, wall-mounted mirror. Spidery cracks slithered from one end where it was broken. Consequently, my reflection was jagged. Distorted. Perhaps it was indicative of the divided self I was becoming by loving a man who wasn't my husband.

Pushing the thought aside, I exited the bathroom and stopped when seeing something I'd obviously missed. A cot covered with blankets was tucked in one corner. I imagined it was where Gabe rested. Where he slept. Clothed. Perhaps naked.

I shook off a wicked tremor even while noting a rifle on the floor beside the cot serving as a bed.

Gabe collected rifles like a hobbyist. As a child his father had taught him how to properly handle their firepower and they'd often hunted together along with his older brothers. Guns were as natural to him as paints were to me. Still, seeing the gun resting there furthered my earlier thought that, perhaps, this space had become home for him.

I'd love to lay on that narrow cot snuggled next to him.

I scurried away, telling myself to pull it together and put on my best innocence like I had good sense, wishing I'd avoided that trip to the storeroom and the temptations it held that I should've avoided.

It took twice as long to paint the Thurmans' storefront window as it had the Graysons. Not because the design was more complicated, but because of Gabe. He was a divine distraction and I couldn't resist the temptation to watch as he interacted with customers or assisted his mother. He was naturally kind and possessed a charm that was simple yet magnetic. I'd always known him to possess a positive temperament, but he moved with a newfound confidence and maturity that I found mesmerizing and appealing. Watching him made my heart yearn for a way to reclaim the time we'd been apart. I wanted the missed moments, the shared laughter, the banter, and even the disagreements. I wanted to sit with him and listen as he told stories of his war experience, as he filled in the gaps of our lost years.

You wanna do more than sit and listen. You wanna make love with him.

That unholy notion sent my hand so far off track that the "F" I was painting could've been a creature from one of Peanut's drawings.

"You'll be here all day painting and repainting Thurman's Fine Furniture if you keep thinking like a hot tail hussy."

Clearly I couldn't work *and* entertain thoughts of Gabe and our sweet reunion, or revisit the kiss we'd shared that proved so tender yet poignant that it felt endless. Doing so was leading me down a track of unacceptable imaginings. Regardless of Willard's conduct, I'd taken vows and that required honorable conduct.

With a rag from my kit I wiped away that mess of an "F" and told myself to concentrate as I returned to my work only to lose my focus when seeing Gabe.

He was near the front counter and leaned against it in a deceptively casual pose. His stare exposed an inward intensity that radiated fiery heat too in keeping with my own scandalous wants and needs. Briefly, I envied his being unattached and wished I, too, was free to love as I pleased. Free or not, the fire between us could incinerate us both beyond repair. There would be no way of reversing anything we unleashed.

That reality squashed every delightful flutter in my belly as I held his gaze and slowly shook my head, denying him as well as myself.

Colemanville was a beautiful place to call home, but it wasn't immune to scandal. A too good Friday night could keep Sheriff Weaver occupied with driving inebriated folks home. Miz Quincy had been banned from the usher board at Evergreen Missionary Baptist Church for pilfering from the offering plate. And Pumpkin Minkins' daughter looked more like the very married Councilman Ashwood than the councilman did himself. In M'Dear's words, humans were human. We could crave, want, and make ridiculous choices from greed. That didn't give me a right to scandalize myself. Or Gabe.

I wanted what we once had with everything within me, but *we* were off limits.

Shaking my head, I wordlessly did my best to convey this. He simply returned my stare, without objection or acceptance, as if he knew something I didn't.

"Auntie Ilona!"

I had my niece, Callie, to thank for pulling me from my divine distraction that could prove dangerous. She raced up the raised wooden walkway with Suda Mae Jackson in tow. The two nearly collided with a customer exiting Mr. and Mrs. Cooper's Tidy Time Laundry. They apologized and continued their happy journey.

"Walk, please." I watched them slow their pace and hugged both when they reached me. "Girls, you can't run on the walkway when people are out and about. You have to be careful not to hurt yourselves or others. You almost knocked Mr. Cooper's customer over."

"Sorry, Auntie Ilona. I guess that's why Uncle Willard called me graceful...no, *graceless* and clumsy."

The idea of Willard aiming criticisms at any child, let alone my favorite niece, stung like pepper sauce on my skin. "Really?"

"Yep. Know what else he said?"

"What?"

Callie glanced at Suda Mae before motioning for me to bend toward her. She cupped her mouth with both hands and whispered in my ear. "He said Suda Mae and me can't be friends."

I avoided looking at Suda Mae to protect the fact that she was the topic of discussion. I mirrored Callie's whisper. "Why not?"

"He said she's stupid and dirty."

I closed my eyes and bit my lip to keep from cussing.

Suda Mae Jackson's family lived two houses down from us. They were sweet, neighborly people and had been nothing but kind since relocating to Colemanville when Suda Mae was three. She and Callie had instantly taken to each other. Any time Callie came to visit us it was only a matter of minutes before she was working her way over to the Jacksons looking for Suda Mae or Suda Mae arrived on our front porch looking for her friend. Their carefree giggles often floated into my art shed, inspiring my color choices, and sometimes my productivity. Willard's evil and unfounded objections were, once again, most likely rooted in not just cruelty, but snobbery.

Mr. Jackson worked at a fishery in Jacksonville. Miz Jackson did domestic labor there as well. Suda Mae had two older brothers, aged eleven and twelve, who were left in charge in their parents' absence. Sometimes the Jacksons returned home late, looking so tired and worn that I often took plates of dinner to them so Miz. Jackson wouldn't have to cook. They always expressed appreciation and went out of their way to return the kindness. Still, Willard looked down his nose at them as if their means of earning a living was appalling.

"Suda Mae, we won't be but a moment." I took Callie's hand and moved away in order to speak softly but freely. "What do you think of your friend? Do *you* think she's dirty or stupid?"

Her little face scrunched up as if she was about to cry as

she rapidly shook her head. "No, ma'am! She's the nicest friend in the whole wide world. And she's even prettier than me. She's just quiet. Like you. That don't make her dumb, does it?"

"It *doesn't* make her dumb at all. And the friendship you two share is a sweet gift."

"Me and Suda Mae plan to still be friends when we're old. Like you and Miss Greenie."

That left me laughing. "Good for the two of you! But what're y'all doing down here to begin with?"

"We're going to the library."

"That's at the end of the street in the opposite direction."

"Well...we just wanted to peek in Miz Grayson's window to see the candy barrels first."

"Suda Mae, come here sweetie." I pulled from my pin money and gave each girl a nickel. "No need to window shop when you have a rich auntie."

Their effusive thanks warmed my heart as I ensured they safely crossed the road to the mercantile. But seeing their safe passage complete, that joy plummeted.

I couldn't recall being so angry. Ever.

The Thurmans' window signage was unfinished, still I snatched up my supplies and stuffed them back in my kit. I'd have to apologize to Miz Thurman for my unprofessionalism and complete the work later. Right then, the anger roaring through me made my energy inappropriate for creating beauty and left my hands unsteady.

"Ilona? What's going on?" Gabe's sudden appearance beside me was startling.

I'd been so immersed in unseemly emotions that I hadn't noticed him exiting the store. His gentle touch on my shoulder would have delighted me another time, another day. Right then it caused me to jerk away from him.

I couldn't tolerate his tenderness. Not when I had a husband like Willard to deal with.

"I'm fine." I didn't look Gabe in the face, knowing he'd see through the lie. Instead, I clutched my belongings tightly and hurried off despite his calling after me.

I hurried toward that footbridge connecting downtown to residential neighborhoods that I'd crossed countless times in life praying for my husband's soul and mine.

"Lord, help me not to kill Willard Brinks."

His criticizing Callie was insulting enough. But speaking of Suda Mae in such a vile way made my blood bake. I stomped home unsure of what I'd do when I got there. But one thing was certain, Willard Brinks wasn't merely elitist and insensitive. He was downright ignorant. And at that moment I was disgusted by the man I'd married and needed him to know precisely how I felt about him.

Fifteen

She's just quiet. Like you. That don't make her dumb, does it?

Callie's words kept me company as I marched toward home. They made me bristle, made me think. Made me wonder if stupid was how Willard saw me, or if he'd mistaken my gentleness for cowardice.

"As if I'm some spineless, pathetic thing to be pushed around and dominated."

My not being loud or raucous, hands on my hips fussing and telling every somebody their business, didn't make me weak, pathetic, or powerless. And I craved a way to help Willard understand that. I also needed him to know his treatment of precious innocents like Callie and Suda Mae wouldn't be tolerated. It was as unacceptable as the way he treated me, the woman he married and should have honored, if not cherished. His constant criticism and disinterest in my art were disheartening, but his acting as if I was physically and intimately loathsome had stabbed at my sense of self more deeply than I cared to admit.

"And I let him." I'd quietly accepted his lack of kindness

and contempt on far too many occasions. "Not anymore, buddy boy. That disrespect stops today!"

Our home was barely two blocks away when I made an unexpected detour down Laurel Lane. It was a Saturday. My visit wasn't expected. I prayed my sudden appearance didn't prove intrusive as I hurried up the walkway, blind to the immaculate yard bordered by a newly painted picket fence. I rang the doorbell of the modest home and waited impatiently until hearing the sound of someone approaching from the opposite side of the door.

"Ilona…I mean, Miz Brinks…what an unexpected but pleasant surprise. Good morning!"

"Good morning, Miz North. Please pardon my interrupting your Saturday. Is Principal North available?"

"Of course he's available to one of his favorite teachers." She pushed the screen door open and waved me forward with a smile.

"Thank you, ma'am. That's kind of you to say." I placed my kit on the porch and followed her indoors. "I promise not to take too much of his time."

"It's no bother at all. Come in and make yourself comfortable in the front parlor. Can I pour you something to drink? We have lemonade or sweet tea."

I declined her graciousness and sat on the edge of an overstuffed chair as she went in search of her husband, appreciating that she took my presence seriously rather than chitchatting. A brief moment later Principal North appeared —tall, angular, and wearing a worried expression.

"Miz Brinks…it's always a pleasure to see you…but what brings you here on a Saturday?"

I stood and accepted his brief, fatherly embrace. "I apologize for the inconvenience—"

"No apology needed. My door is always open to the fine

staff of Colemanville Elementary. I'm just surprised, is all. Is anything amiss?"

I knew him to be a kind, efficient, no-nonsense leader whose commitment to our school's welfare was always apparent. I relied on those attributes as I followed his indication to take a seat.

"I wanted to request that going forward my paychecks be given to me directly and no longer to Mr. Brinks."

"Well...yes...of course as you wish. We only distributed them to him based on yours...or rather his...directives." He was quiet a moment before clearing his throat. "Clearly, something has changed..."

Yes, I woke up and smelled my stupidity.

I nodded without offering additional comment.

Thankfully he didn't press the issue. "I'll notify Miss Evans. She's an efficient secretary and will see to it immediately."

Relief washed over me as I answered his inquiries about my parents' wellbeing before thanking him for his time and leaving. I was no less determined, yet lighter in step as I made a second detour and headed toward my sister Viola's house. Between my three sisters still residing in Colemanville, Viola was the most likely to agree with what I needed. My head lifted a little higher knowing these were first but necessary steps to reclaiming the independence I'd falsely forfeited in the name of marriage.

"Ilona, where've you been?"

I ignored Willard in favor of focusing on my father seated in his wheelchair at the dining room table, an odd but peaceful expression on his face. Perhaps he felt better, stronger today. He'd never been demonstrative. Still, I took advantage of his improved state of being and kissed his forehead, granting myself time to harness my feelings without responding to my husband.

I shrugged off my sweater and draped it across a chair while looking at my mother. "Father seems to be in good spirits."

"And you appear to have gone deaf!"

"Ilona, your husband asked you a question. I'd also like to know as well. Where in the good Lord's name have you been so early on a Saturday?"

I stared at Mother seated beside my father feeling as if I were seeing for the first time the true depths of the manner in which his stroke had caused her to change. Such changes had positioned her on the cusp of being unrecognizable. Whispers of the beautiful woman she once was were still evident in her countenance, but they were subdued by a veil of weariness. Caring for Father in his illness had impacted her, altering more than her visage. It had affected her tolerance, patience, and in some ways her kindness. She was often irritable and perpetually tired. I knew how the sacrifices and demands of marriage could alter a person, and my compassion flowed toward her in that moment.

Compassion's one thing. Standing up for myself is another.

My shoulders lifted as did my resistance against any typical acquiescence. I could acknowledge my mother's sacrifices and state of being without dishonoring or sacrificing myself. "I went to town...to paint signage for the Graysons—"

"Paint? *Signage?*" Willard looked dumbfounded and peeved. "Your playing in paint left me here making breakfast when domestic chores aren't mine to do. They're yours."

I looked at the untouched, unappetizing, slightly charred food on the plates in front of my parents before glancing at Willard's, noting his was empty.

"I'm glad you were able to tolerate the meal you made." He sputtered a bit as I pressed on. "As for signage, weren't you in agreement a few days ago when we were walking home from work and saw Miz Grayson outside her store? I believe your words were somewhere in the neighborhood of I'd gladly oblige her. So, this morning I did."

Willard pushed away from the table. "Being somewhere other than where you should be doing worthless things without anyone knowing is unacceptable. As is your tone."

As is your singular relationship with pornographic photos.

I inhaled deeply to keep from blurting his filth in my parents' presence, as well as to reinforce my courage and my decision as I gave them my focus.

"Mother...Father..." I included Willard by glancing in his direction. "I'm aware we hold dissimilar points of view about my art...but I'm traveling to Raleigh next weekend." I'd never been one for deceitfulness and no longer felt a need for it. Rather, I chose to speak truthfully about my whereabouts for the upcoming weekend. Quickly and succinctly I shared news of The Nubian-Kush Collaborative and its importance to me. "I'm a finalist for an art fellowship and I've been invited to submit a final piece—"

"Wait one dag blasted minute!" Willard jumped to his feet. "What do you *mean* by saying you're going to Raleigh next weekend?"

His failure to offer congratulations wasn't surprising.

I stared at him, angry yet feeling at fault for his ugly disposition toward Suda Mae. Perhaps my accepting his behavior over the years had reinforced his arrogance and insensitivity that had increased to an alarming degree.

"I'll only be gone for the day so my absence shouldn't be a disruption."

Willard interrupted yet again, aggravated as a hornets' nest. "It most definitely is a disruption. To this household. To your parents. And most of all to me!"

I quieted my voice simply to keep from screaming. "I

stopped by Viola's on the way home. Theodora happened to be there, and both agreed to provide whatever assistance may be needed."

I chose not to repeat Theodora's opinion.

According to my fifty-four-year-old eldest sister, my trip to Raleigh was a "superfluous indulgence." Dutiful wives didn't gallivant about the countryside. Home was where I needed to be, helping Mother tend to Father, and ensuring the creature comforts of my husband.

I'd shouldered her subsequent rebuke and simply reiterated that my trip was definite. If Theodora was unwilling or unable to help Viola in checking on our parents, I'd simply ask our other sister, Olivia, knowing that my three oldest siblings —grown and in their fifties—still loved an opportunity to outdo each other. No way on God's green earth would our oldest sister allow the younger Olivia to show herself more devout or devoted. That sealed her agreement and silenced her resistance.

"Ilona, dear, traveling isn't safe. Not with all the racial unrest from that Peekskill riot."

Two months ago, in August, a civil rights benefit concert was violently interrupted by a gang of white folks objecting to the concert's headliner. Famed African-American actor and renaissance man, Paul Robeson, was a communist sympathizer who didn't hold his tongue on U.S. policies abroad or stateside. His inclusion in the event proved a perfect excuse for white violence and protest.

I almost smiled at my mother's weak attempt to dissuade me. "Mother, I'll be a few miles away in Raleigh, not New York. Everything will be fine. I promise."

"And who exactly do you think is paying for this frivolous excursion? I most certainly am not."

I'd expected as much from Willard and took pleasure in my response. "I need nothing from you. I'll manage."

He slammed a fist on the dining room table so fiercely that my father jerked backwards and began coughing violently.

"Enough, Ilona! You're upsetting your father's constitution."

I swallowed the retort on my lips that Willard was the one pounding the table like an ignoramus. Where was her censure for him?

Mother was notorious for cautioning me against negatively affecting my father's health, trotting out such admonitions if ever I failed to comply with a command as quickly as she wished or if I broached a subject she preferred not to deal with. I refused to let her tactics deter me as we both rushed to Father's aid to help him drink from the water glass beside his plate.

He managed a few sips before waving us away.

"He's had enough, Ilona. We all have. We understand that art is important to you, but we've discussed this time and again. Life as an artist...particularly for a Colored woman...is unproductive. So, please, discontinue this notion of traveling somewhere by yourself, especially for such a silly and impulsive reason."

I ignored the tiny stab in my stomach caused by her dismissiveness. She'd had me in her later years, but the distance separating us was more than age. We were separated by a tumultuous ocean of misunderstanding churning with a difference of opinion. "It's neither impulsive nor silly to me, Mother, it's—"

Father suddenly flopped his good arm up and down, arresting our attention and preventing me from finishing.

He indicated a writing implement with his thumb and forefinger. "Get...paper..."

Mother waved a hand toward the kitchen. "His pad and pen are in there."

I retrieved both quickly. Positioning the pad before him, I attempted to help him grip the ink pen but he waved me away.

"Can do...myself..."

Willard leaned forward, attempting to read from the opposite side of the table, only for Father to grant him a withering stare that caused him to retreat.

"What is he writing?"

Father ignored Willard's question and pointed at me, then the front of the house before resuming.

"Good Lord, Jonah, what is all this?"

Father answered Mother's inquiry by grabbing my hand and placing it atop the pad.

Lifting the pad, I gave little attention to the fact that Father's handwriting had been reduced to what M'Dear would have called chicken scratch. I focused, instead, on the rebelliousness in what he'd communicated.

"Well...what did he say?"

Willard's tone was demanding, peevish.

Father nodded at me, confirming his intent, as I turned the pad in Willard's direction allowing him to read for himself.

Go my blessing

"What does that mean, Father Robertson?"

I answered for him. "My father is in favor of my going to Raleigh."

"He absolutely is *not*!" Willard looked to Jonah Robertson as if needing reinforcement of his selfish perspective and found the opposite instead.

Again, Father indicated me, then the front of the house as if directing me to leave. "Ilona's...art's...important... She goes..."

The eternity it took for my father to offer an opinion I'd never heard from him was more than worth it. Every word was like a drop of soothing ointment falling on parched places and caused my chest to expand with emotion. I wanted to thank him profusely but Willard's brewing discontent took precedence.

My husband glared at me as if at a mortal enemy. He opened his mouth with objections but my father shook his head, curtailing them.

Willard stomped from the room, leaving what felt like an icy ribbon of contempt trailing behind him.

Mother rose from her seat and properly folded her linen napkin before placing it on the table. She gripped the handles of Father's wheelchair tightly. "I taught my daughters to respect and honor their husbands. Not feud with and challenge them privately or publicly. Apparently, I didn't do my job thoroughly enough."

I moved aside and watched her wheel Father from the room as if getting away from me was paramount to their sanity. Even so, I experienced an odd elation. My mother's rebuke couldn't stand up to my father's approval and acceptance. I felt heard. Seen.

Eyes closed, I let delight wash over me. With Father's blessing, a week from today, I was headed for Raleigh.

Sixteen

Jonah Robertson supported my decision!

Buoyed by the thrill of it, I wanted to skip down the back porch steps to my art shed like Callie and Suda Mae skipping through downtown earlier that day. I'd never asked much of my parents. Because of their advanced age, I'd grown up knowing that, as a dutiful and devoted daughter, our roles might one day reverse and that I'd be caring for them in their later years. I was grateful for them and didn't object to this, in fact, now being my reality. I'd returned home after college graduation, married the man of their choice, and daily gave myself to their needs. All I'd hoped for in return was their loving support and acknowledgement of my gift and talent. Now, I had that. At least from one parent.

"Father's support is a long awaited gift from heaven."

No matter how much I craved my mother's blessing, I chose to release any hope that she would one day embrace or even make room in her heart for my gift. I'd been raised to honor my elders, my parents, and had never blatantly disrespected either of them; that didn't mean I agreed with Mother's every opinion. At times, I considered her approach to life old-fashioned, particularly her penchant for impeccable decorum and the overly formal. It was evident in her prim fashion sense. Being called "mother" instead of a diminutive. Her strict requirement for a pristine home that could pass a white glove test.

My mother is rigid.

Even so, I offered grace in the face of her rigidities knowing some were rooted in history.

She told stories of her own grandmother, mother of my beloved M'Dear, having been enslaved; and the struggles she endured after emancipation to create a viable life for herself and her seven children. Her fight wasn't merely for economic wellbeing, freedom, and safety, but for dignity. Consequently, M'Dear had raised her own children to be mannerly, polite, and to live honorable lives. Mother required the same of us, but with an unyielding and often heavy touch.

But that day I'd experienced the pure delight of motherly women in Miz Thurman and Miz Grayson. They saw my gift, even vied for it, and that in tandem with my father's favor left me feeling as if a lifetime of weight had been lifted as I neared my art shed.

That effervescent feeling fizzled at the sight of my art shed door standing ajar. The padlock I used to keep my work secure lay on the ground, cut away by hedge clippers now leaning against the side of the shed. Ignoring an ominous sensation slithering down my back, I silently entered my sacred space only to encounter a disaster I hadn't created.

My easel and smock lay on the floor. Canvases and my supply caddies had been knocked over. Paint dripped from an overturned container now missing its lid. The sound of its steady plopping seemed in sync with my racing heartbeat. I saw and heard, still it was as if I was momentarily suspended in a fog of disbelief as I stared at the man who'd made mayhem of what was precious to me.

"Willard! What're you doing?" My horrified scream filled the space, causing him to whirl in my direction.

His face was tight, his stance unyielding. "You're hiding something and I plan to find out exactly what it is and where."

"Get out of my workshop!" I hurried toward him, wanting to prevent further damage, except he was already busy ransacking my wall-mounted shelves. "Willard, what is wrong with you? Stop it!" I grabbed his shoulder, trying to curtail the destruction.

He shrugged me off. "Where is it?"

"Where is *what*?"

He thrust a hand out, ignoring me. "Your pay."

"Excuse me?"

"You heard me clearly, Ilona. Your earnings! I'll have whatever money you made painting windows today."

My mouth hung open in disbelief as I stared at his outstretched palm before raising my gaze to his, feeling as if we'd both slipped into a whirlpool of madness. "I need you to leave. Now, Willard."

"Are you disobeying me?" Shock registered on his face.

"You're neither God nor my father. So call it disobeying you if you wish, but yes. It looks like I am."

"Give me the money, Ilona."

I shook my head, saddened by our sad state of affairs. "You're far too controlling, Willard, and I can't continue this marriage in this manner. I'm naturally generous but my generosity doesn't equal stupidity. Whatever I earn through art belongs to me." I inhaled hungrily as if the air was laced with courage. "I'm always willing to share and to continue contributing to our needs...but just so you know, I informed Principal North that going forward my wages are to come to me directly—"

"You did what?" His eyes bulged in disbelief.

I stood my ground even as he stepped ominously toward me. "I will no longer endorse my paychecks over to you."

"As the man of this house—"

"We live with my parents. We'd have to have a house in order for you to be the man of it. And why, exactly, haven't we bought our own residence yet? We do nothing *but* save." Our expenses were few and Willard limited our outings, finding movies and such pastimes as wasteful. "Haven't we accumulated enough for a down payment?"

Even as I asked the question I didn't care to hear the response. It saddened me to realize my heart wasn't present, that I no longer wanted to buy a house or build a home with this person. That truth left me feeling so raw and hopeless that I had to escape it and focused elsewhere. "Did you tell Callie that Suda Mae Jackson was ugly and dirty?"

"I spoke only the truth."

Sadness coated my heart. I felt ashamed that I was tied to this less than loving individual. "You're a cruel person, Willard Brinks."

"Cruel?" He sputtered and stuttered incoherently until regaining his faculties. "You know nothing about cruel, with your padded and perfect upbringing. Cruel is being given one meal each day, being beaten for any grade less than an A, and awakened every morning at four a.m. to pray on your knees three hours before school."

"Was that your experience?"

"Enough of this! Something's gotten into you and whatever it is I highly dislike it." He dismissed me and resumed his wreckage.

I rushed toward him, stopping abruptly as he carelessly snatched my treasured box with the delicate hummingbird painted on its lid. I forced myself not to yank it from his grasp to avoid his becoming fixated on it or it being damaged.

Anger coursed through me when he carelessly flung open the lid and scavenged through its contents until landing on my award letter from The Kush Nubian Art Collaborative.

Scanning it quickly, he gripped it between his fingertips and held it in the air as if it were toxic.

"*This* is what's gotten into you and I forbid your participation!" He dropped the letter into the carved box and closed the lid only to suddenly reopen it. Repositioning his glasses, he leaned in and ran a plump finger over the engraved heart and initials that decorated the inner lid.

"I.R. plus G.T." He read the engraving out loud in a way that made me cringe. His tone was lewd. Suggestive. "Ilona Robertson is obvious. Who is G.T.?"

I wanted to slap the smug superiority from his face as he crossed his arms and turned toward me.

I said nothing.

"Hiding that art fellowship nonsense is one thing, but I will *never* tolerate infidelity."

"I made that box when I was in high school—"

"I don't care! I deplore secrets and falsehoods and the liars who keep them. Especially whores and adulteresses."

I drew back as if I'd been slapped. His words stung and I retaliated by spewing my thoughts before I could swallow them. "And what about husbands with pornographic postcards stashed beneath bathroom sinks?"

The sound of the autumn wind filled the space our sudden silence created. Silence sat heavily between us for interminable seconds that felt like minutes until I broke it.

"I know about your naked pictures, Willard." A curious and unwanted compassion shot through me. I was suddenly disinterested in humiliating him and spoke with a tenderness he didn't deserve and failed to show others. My husband, however, failed to reciprocate the same grace.

He grabbed the arm I'd injured when falling off my bike

the other day. I struggled against his grasp but he squeezed so mercilessly that my eyes watered from the pain.

"How dare you accuse me of such degeneracy!"

"Auntie Ilona..."

My heart dropped seeing Callie standing in the doorway. I wasn't sure how much she'd observed, but the look on her face indicated she'd witnessed enough to be frightened.

Willard released me immediately and I rushed toward my niece.

She ran to me and wrapped her arms about my waist.

"Hey, sweetie..."

"Why was Uncle Willard yelling?"

"Everything's okay." I offered that lie and held her close, stroking her thick, neat plaits secured at the ends with pretty little yellow and white ribbons. She trembled as she clung to me. I hated that she was upset and kissed the top of her head and reassured her again. "Did Suda Mae come with you?"

She looked at Willard in a way that indicated a fear of his reaction. She shook her head and buried her face against me as he stalked toward the door.

He paused before exiting, casting a command over his shoulders without looking back. "Ilona...don't forget the painting I requested for Principal North. I'll need it by next Thursday...please."

I praised God as he left, thankful that worse hadn't happened.

I smiled to hide my vexation and sorrow from my niece, but I wanted to pray, light a candle, and purge my sacred space of vile energy and unclean spirits. My art shed was my refuge, my haven, and it was imperative to me that it be filled with peace. This encounter with Willard had altered its purity.

"Seems like Uncle Willard's always mad at somebody and don't...I mean *doesn't* like nobody. Sometimes he acts like he doesn't even like you, Auntie."

Callandra's grasp of the man I'd married left me speechless and disheartened to think the disharmony of our union was obvious even to a child. Her simple honesty was like a brisk wind, blowing away any remaining disillusionment or pretense I might have been clutching.

My husband doesn't love me. I don't love him. He's a sick, abusive, and miserable person.

"Out of the mouth of babes comes wit and wisdom."

"Huh?"

"It just means you're super smart, Callie. But we already knew that. Right?"

She giggled when I pulled one of her plaits. "What happened to your studio, Aunt Ilona?"

A husband hurricane.

I held her hand as we assessed the mess Willard made. I wanted to cry seeing how my sanctuary had been desecrated, but put on a brave face for Callie's benefit. "Would you like to help me clean it up? We can do watercolor painting when we finish."

"Sure! Oh...wait..." She pulled a folded scrap of paper from her sweater pocket and handed it to me.

"What's this?" I closed my eyes and pressed the paper to my forehead, pretending to guess its content. "Is it the secret code to some ancient mystery? Wait...I believe it's a recipe for toadstool cookies."

"No, Auntie!" Her laughter was like fresh rain after the storm I'd just experienced. "It's from Mr. Gator. He gave it to me when I was downtown with Suda Mae when we went back to Miz Grayson's to spend the rest of our candy money after the library."

A lightning bolt of heat pulsed through me and my playfulness disappeared.

"He told me don't let nobody see it but you. Did I do good?"

I tore my attention from the paper long enough to answer. "Of course you did."

She smiled and released my hand to busy herself with the task before us. "Come on, Aunt Ilona. We gotta clean. When we finish I'ma paint a masterpiece and give it to Suda Mae 'cause she likes pretty things."

"That's very nice of you, Callie. I'm sure Suda Mae will love whatever you create." I watched my niece carefully reclaim the items Willard had treated with disregard just to avoid the note cradled in the palm of my hand as memories of what transpired between Gabe and I that morning rose with delicious, shameful torment.

That note I held was precious yet dangerous. I was torn between reading with the same desperation as a dying woman gulping oxygen or ripping it to shreds. The former prevailed.

Grotto Galleria.

Had Callie accidentally dropped that note in anyone's presence, even Willard's, no one would have been the wiser as to its meaning. Grotto Galleria didn't exist. At least not for anyone except me. And Gabe.

Seventeen

Colemanville was mostly flat land with minor variations in elevation that created a spattering of small hills guarded by statuesque trees, mainly white oaks and elms. Not so on the back side of town near Packer's family's land where their horses roamed freely. That landscape was decidedly different. There, gentle hills rolled with graceful ease. Even valleys existed.

Nestled in the small bowl of one valley was a cave. At least that was what I'd called it the first time Gabe introduced me to it the summer of our high school graduation. It was on one of those rare occasions when we'd managed to sneak away from the condemning eyes of my parents.

You've gotta see it, Sweet Rivers. It's a whole underground wonderland. You gotta paint it!

His excitement proved contagious, pushing me past my hesitations and into the dark cavern. I'd clutched his hand so tightly he claimed his bones were breaking as we cautiously proceeded with a flashlight's faint illumination. He'd warned me in advance of bats hanging overhead, still—coming in sight of their small, distended forms—I'd had to cover my mouth to avoid yelling and waking them. Enduring any terror they incited was worth the treasure that waited within.

Stalactites and stalagmites decorated the ceiling and sprouted from the earth like magical, icy looking crystals unlike anything I'd ever seen. Colorful prisms danced gracefully about the walls of the cavern as we shone the flashlight on them. It was beautiful. Majestic. And Gabe was oh so accurate in that I *had* to paint them.

Buying art supplies with my allowance and storing them in the cave proved easier than anticipated. Sneaking away, however, proved challenging until Greenie and I landed on a deception. Every Wednesday afternoon I claimed to be with her, helping on her family's farm. I showed up long enough to validate my presence on the off chance that Greenie's or my parents happened to discuss it. But within minutes of my arrival, I was in the wind, rushing to meet Gabe in our mystical, magical kingdom.

I painted so many variations of that precious place that Gabe teasingly called it my underground gallery. At the time he was fascinated by foreign language and world travel, specifically Italy. That was how he landed on Grotto Galleria when naming the space where we wanted to give each other our virginity. Only the fear of a possible pregnancy preventing me from going to college curtailed passion's fulfillment. Instead, we lay on a blanket gazing at the crystals overhead–touching, kissing, and imagining a future that included a marriage bed.

Years had passed since then. Yet, I felt an intense yearning for the innocent intimacy of our youth thanks to the note cradled in the palm of my hand. It was a summons, an invitation to revisit an enchanted part of our history. It was also dangerous.

"I can't."

Not after kissing Gabe and tasting a fleeting shadow of pleasure. Not with the sad condition of my marriage.

I had no way of knowing precisely why Gabe sent the note and chose not to be presumptuous or assign meaning to his intentions. I knew him to be an honorable man who wouldn't compromise me. Yet, I recognized my vulnerabilities, and that I was too starved for affection. Being alone in the presence of my first love in a secluded place that held precious memories was not in my best interest. And while the state of my relationship with Willard worried me immensely, I felt torn between finding a way to make it work and doing the unthinkable and simply walking away. I was raised to be a wife for life. The notion of divorce wasn't something to be entertained. Yet I knew it was impossible for us to continue in our present condition. The state of our union dangled on a thin and unstable thread, and I was beginning to question the state of Willard's mental wellness.

"He can *never* enter my art space...or mishandle me again."

I couldn't stomach physical violence and his repeatedly grabbing me, lately, was far from acceptable. Vows be damned.

Vows be damned...

For a millisecond of a moment I permitted myself to imagine stepping away from vows that seemed meaningless in order to love and be loved by Gabe in return only to experience an unwelcome stab of conscience.

"Lord, it can never happen."

Shredding the note Callie gave me earlier that day, I let the pieces flutter onto my side table and looked about my art shed. With her help, order had been restored. All things were in their proper places. Only my heart felt like a mosaic of shattered glass in complete disarray as I wrapped my arms about myself and bitterly wept until my entire soul ached.

My fingers were sufficient to count the words Willard grunted in my presence from the afternoon he ravaged my sacred space to the time we arrived at the Harvest Festival two days later that Monday evening. He'd avoided me all weekend, practically sleeping on the edge of the bed, sitting tightly in church to avoid our touching. If he meant to hurt me, he didn't. His sullen silence and avoidance was a godsend. Certainly his behavior created tension, but the absence of his voice and opinion was a much needed gift of peace. It was the kind of peace I hadn't possessed in years and didn't fully realize how desperately I missed it until experiencing it again. It was in this sweet serenity that boldness blossomed within, whispering a contrary yet liberating truth that I could no longer tolerate the facade Willard and I called marriage.

"What're you gonna do, LoLo?"

Greenie's words were a near whisper as we stood side-by-side behind the dessert table serving happy children Monday night. The Harvest Festival was in full effect on the back lawn of First Jubilee AME that had been transformed into a veritable carnival. There was food, games, and other delightful offerings, including but not limited to ring toss, a puppet show, bobbing for apples and, my favorite, Pin the Tail on the Devil. In between handing out candied apples, caramel corn, cotton candy, and licorice whips, I'd quietly confessed the unfortunate state of my affairs to my dearest friend. Willard's demanding I forge a painting. His manhandling me. Even his pornographic pastime. I admitted the unhappiness I'd lived with, holding nothing back, except the resurgence of my love for Gabriel.

It might have seemed cowardly or imprudent of me to divulge such things in a public space, but my heart was too raw to hold the outpour of Greenie's sorrow and outrage that would have erupted had our conversation taken place in a private setting.

Here, I could control my emotions and help curtail hers in

this festive environment where laughing children served as a balm to my aching spirit.

"I'm not sure, Greenie. All I know is I can't be married to Willard. Not like this," I added. It was an afterthought, like a final attempt despite the notion pressing on my heart and mind that any and all connections to my husband needed to end.

"Ever thought about the two of you talking to someone... maybe Pastor Isaacson?"

I shrugged. "I doubt that'll help much." Pastor Isaacson was a profound teacher of God's Word, but he also leaned toward patriarchy and wives submitting to their husbands in all things without mention of whether or not said husbands were honorable and deserving. "I should've listened to you way back when."

LoLo, take your time with that man. Something ain't right about him.

I'd acknowledged the concerns she expressed when Greenie first met Willard. And I *had* taken my time. Two whole years.

Coming home after college graduation, I'd waited for Gabe to return from the war, to come back to Colemanville and back to us despite my parents attempts to steer my affections elsewhere. His family had informed me of his injury. I was prepared to love him the same, not less. With everything within me I was determined to show him it didn't reduce him as a man. Even when his letters ceased, I held onto hope that he'd find the courage to return to a love that I prayed could help heal him. But he never did. Out of patience and at his wit's end, my father insisted on Willard as my life partner. I defied his wishes. It proved a clashing encounter that ended in a stroke that nearly caused his death, and at times I was still haunted by it.

Greenie reached for my hand and held it gently. "Honey,

we're not gonna do shoulda, woulda, *or* coulda. You did what you thought was best."

"And I regret it."

"Yeah...well...listen. If you wanna get away and clear your head and let your thinking get straight, come bunk out with me for a few days."

It wasn't the same as going away and having time beyond the borders of Colemanville. But it was a wonderful idea and a chance to think my way through some things in a peaceful environment free from marital strife and the daily demands of my father's health and the dreariness of domesticity. The mere thought of sharing Greenie's company was absolutely enticing and brightened my heart instantly.

"I wouldn't be an imposition?"

"Girl, no! You gonna earn your keep working my fields with me."

Our blended laughter felt sweet, further lifting me. But only momentarily. As if pulled by sources unseen, my attention drifted to the far side of the expansive lawn to land on a new arrival. I watched him weave his way through the crowd, pausing here and there to greet neighbors and friends. I looked on with hurt and hunger until our eyes connected across the distance with a force that felt powerful, magnetic.

I watched as his shoulders squared briefly before softening like a sail without wind. The desolate expression he tried but failed to hide left me feeling traitorous.

Forgive me for failing you.

I'd failed him by not showing up at our Grotto Galleria as invited, and my heart cried the words I longed for him to hear as he held my gaze and headed in my direction only to be accosted by Pumpkin Minkins manifesting seemingly out of nowhere. The woman was smoother than oil as she sidled next to him. She threw me hateful glances while doing her damndest to steer him in a different direction.

Her efforts proved ineffective as he continued toward me with Pumpkin trotting behind him with her non-stop chattering.

"You never stopped loving Gabe."

I was too emotionally exhausted to contradict Greenie's statement. Unable to divert my focus from the man coming toward me, I simply nodded and wished for a way to reverse time and undo the choices I'd made. "I should've waited."

"Waited for what?" Willard was suddenly in front of the dessert table loaded with sweets he didn't need.

My face warmed as I snatched my gaze from Gabe and Pumpkin, hoping my husband was ignorant to the object of my focus. But he wasn't. I'd always known Willard Brinks to be shrewd and observant and felt immobilized as he turned to see what, rather who, had seized my attention.

The four of us stood as if suspended in a strange tableau. Gabe. Pumpkin. Willard. And me. My heart raced and my hands were suddenly clammy. I could only pray Willard wouldn't perceive the longing and love that had resurfaced between Gabe and me.

I was certain her actions weren't anywhere near altruistic, still I could have kissed Pumpkin when she smiled and waved, causing Willard to focus on her. Not Gabe.

"Willard, we have candied apples and caramel corn? Would you like to try some?"

Greenie's inquiry provided further distraction, releasing me from paralysis.

I busied myself serving my husband sugary treats he didn't need, thanking God I'd escaped a situation that could have been disastrous.

"Thank you." Willard's tone was terse as he accepted the treats I offered him. "I've had my fill of the festival. There are far too many children." His nose wrinkled in disgust. "I'm headed home."

"That's fine. I'll finish out the evening and catch a ride with Greenie."

To her place. Not ours.

I kept that to myself as he added a second caramel apple to his stash and left.

Exhaling a sigh of relief, I desperately searched for Gabe. He was nowhere to be seen. I found Pumpkin Minkins instead.

She stood mere feet away, her expression malicious.

"That child looks like she wanna toss daggers at your head. She must still be upset over you suggesting something more sane than burlesque dancing at last Friday's DOLLs meeting."

Greenie was sharp. Attentive. Not mentioning the four-way disaster that had almost happened was her being gracious. Not ignorant. Clearly, my dearest friend intuited I needed time to navigate what felt like an impossible maze. I wanted to thank her for sensitivity but was diverted by an eerie sensation scurrying over my skin as Pumpkin waved again, her mouth upturned in what I could only describe as a calculating and devious grin.

I looked away to serve a group of children approaching the table and asking for cotton candy, wondering if I needed blessed oil *and* the blood of Jesus.

Eighteen

"LoLo, this feels a little like our last sleepover."

I tightened my coat against a slight drizzle and the evening breeze as we exited Old Faithful and headed toward our front walkway.

"Greenie, our last sleepover was the weekend before my wedding. This is different." Back then I wanted to run away. Rather than submit to such drastic actions I'd blamed cold feet for the cautionary jitters I experienced versus admitting the truth that I was making a mistake. Three years later I now had the same burning desire to escape. "Come to think of it, this *is* about the same."

Time had passed but, in this regard, very little had changed. Here I was intent on packing an overnight bag and heading to Greenie's because of the state of my marriage.

But you've changed. You have choice and experience.

I clung to hope and the belief that both would work in my favor as I opened the front gate.

I wasn't the same lovesick, naive, and inexperienced young woman waiting on Gabe like Penelope for Odysseus. Shifts were occurring within and I felt myself moving away from errant notions of duty and obligation that had limited my existence. It was simultaneously frightening and liberating.

Wanting it desperately doesn't mean it isn't unnerving.

It was, yet I told myself I was ready. I'd been spared a horrible collision earlier that evening, in diverting Willard's attention and escaping any accusations of impropriety. Still, the draw between Gabe and I was too intense to forever go unnoticed and I didn't want to be embroiled in anything sordid.

I stopped mid-stride at a pounding sound coming from the rear of the house.

"What in the world is that?"

I laughed at Greenie grabbing my coat sleeve and pressing against me. "The outhouse door. The latch is faulty."

"Well, somebody needs to fix that thing. It's breezy but not *that* windy. In fact, when're y'all gonna get around to razing that monstrosity?"

I put a finger to my lips as I headed in that direction with Greenie still clutching my coat. I whispered a response. "I'll see about getting it torn down when I get back from Raleigh. For now, lemme just latch the door before all that banging wakes everyone."

I tiptoed past our bedroom window, praying Willard was lost deep in sleep as he tended to be after a full day of work and any added activities. I nearly felt guilty with relief knowing the festivities of the Harvest Festival would have added to his dead-to-the-world exhaustion.

If you're leaving, leave like a grown, choice-having woman.

I lifted my head and straightened my spine and took the advice of the voice I now associated with our Lady Liberty. It was gentle. Sweet. It imbued me with a powerful assurance that I had no need to sneak anywhere, even Greenie's. If Willard awakened as I packed an overnight bag, so be it. My concern was not putting Greenie in the middle of any unpleasantness that might erupt between me and my husband.

I stopped near the back porch, intending to suggest it might be best for her to wait in Old Faithful, but sounds filtered into the night and snatched our attention.

We stared at each other, alarm on our faces as inhuman noises slithered on the night breeze. They were inhuman yet somehow indicative of physical suffering.

"Oh, hell no! We're going home." Greenie immediately turned in the opposite direction.

I grabbed her sleeve and clutched her hand to keep her from bolting before glancing about the dark night for something, anything to use as protection.

The hedge trimmers used to destroy the padlock that secured my art shed still leaned against its wall where Willard left them. I snatched them up and tiptoed toward the source of the painfilled and disturbing noises, forcing Greenie to move right along with me. The closer we got, the more alarmed we became until coming to a standstill just beyond the outhouse perimeter.

The door was closed, secured against the wind. Instead, the rickety structure wobbled in a way that threatened its viable continuance.

I stared, wide-eyed, at Greenie. The once distant sounds were now distinct. And clearly human.

Without thought I pulled my hand from Greenie's and yanked the door open.

Nothing and no one could have prepared me for the sight of Willard's bare behind pumping with more energy than I knew he possessed until he froze as the cool night air against his naked skin registered in his consciousness.

His head whirled and he looked over his shoulder, glasses cockeyed on his face, to find the unwanted sight of me and Greenie.

"What in heaven!"

Frantically, he reached for the pants pooled about his ankles. Struggling to pull them up and back out of the outhouse simultaneously, he stumbled backwards onto his plump behind.

"Ilona, what in God's name is the meaning of this? Why're you here?"

I wanted to tell him God had nothing to do with his humping in an outhouse like a horny canine as he struggled to his feet, but I was too shocked by the bountiful behind of his copulating partner to say or do anything.

She seemed to relish her exhibition, undulating as if Willard were still in her. She took her slow time releasing her bent over position, raising her bloomers, and lowering the hem of her dress before turning to face us. Unfazed as if this were nothing beyond the norm, she slowly stepped from the outhouse and into the night wearing a sly smile that morphed oddly angelic beneath the moonlight.

"Ilona...darling...go inside. I'll explain later. There's nothing to see here!"

I ignored my husband and watched Pumpkin Minkins stride past Willard without an inch or ounce of shame to her name. She paused when nearing me and leaned in whispering.

"I couldn't get the man we both wanted, so I thought I'd try the one you had instead."

She straightened her posture, speaking loud enough for all assembled to hear. "And your hubby's correct. Ain't nothing to see or feel here. Honey, I don't know how you tolerated that little bit all these years."

She sashayed away, leaving scents of her time with Willard and overly sweet perfume in the night air.

I didn't bother to watch her departure. Instead, I glued my focus on my unfaithful husband.

"Greenie...thank you for bringing my wife home. I'll take it from here."

He reached for me. I jerked away, sickened by what I'd seen. "You'll take it from nowhere! Do *not* touch me. Ever again. As long as you breathe."

"I will *not* be spoken to in such a way."

"I'll speak to you however the hell I please!"

"As your husband, I deserve—"

"The only thing you deserve is having that thing snipped!" He scurried backwards as I brandished the hedge clippers I suddenly remembered I still held.

"*Ilona*. No!" Greenie grabbed me, wrapping her arms about me from behind.

"You are vile. Disgusting. Moralless. And you have ten seconds to leave my parents' property, Willard Brinks, and never come back."

"I will do no such thing!"

"Eight seconds. Keep talking."

He opened his mouth as if fat meat wasn't greasy or he was unaware that my sanity had tipped toward crazy. I lunged for him. Only Greenie's hold and his being beyond arm's reach spared Willard from becoming one with the pointed end of the hedge trimmer.

He scuttled sideways, avoiding impalement and made a cocky attempt at courage. "Fine. I'll leave for now. Only to allow you to calm down."

Greenie held onto me as he walked away only for Willard to suddenly pause as if remembering something. He turned toward us, fixing the glasses on his face while moving in my direction.

"I know who G.T. is. Pumpkin told me all about you and Gator Thurman." He lifted his head in a display of arrogance. "I've been nothing but good to you and can't fathom your need to play the whore, but I do understand your misguided predilection for the poor and needy. A pathetic one-armed man must be a nice bit of charity."

I reacted without thinking, punching Willard in his face with more fury than I knew I possessed.

He plummeted like a sack of bricks.

"Let's go, Greenie. We're finished here." I grabbed her hand and stepped over my husband clutching his bloodied nose, writhing and moaning.

Bypassing the back door, I headed to Old Faithful at a pace that had Greenie nearly trotting.

"LoLo, aren't you going inside to get your things?"

"No." I propped the hedge trimmers against the front gate. "I need to leave before I kill Willard Brinks."

"How's that feel?"

"Like I might need to see Doc Everett." The towel-wrapped ice cubes secured against my hand helped lessen the aftermath of punching my husband. My knuckles felt raw, achy. But I'd suffer it again if it meant being done with him.

"I pray nothing's broken."

"I pray he packed his bags and is catching the next thing smoking." I stared at the steam rising from the cup of chamomile tea Greenie placed in front of me as she seated herself on the opposite side of the table, shaking her head in disbelief.

"LoLo...I'm...shocked and appalled. I wouldn't have believed it if I hadn't seen it myself. With Pumpkin of all people! And in *an outhouse*? That's a low down dirt level of disgusting I hope I never understand."

All I could offer was, "Amen."

Our short trip to Greenie's had been in stunned, angry silence with us glancing at each other every few seconds, mouths open. Now, since being seated in her cheery kitchen,

I'd run an obstacle course of emotions. Rage. Disgust. Disbelief. But nothing remotely resembling the sadness or sorrow associated with the dissolution of a marriage.

Lord, may I be honest and say that I feel free?

I refused to deny the glimmers of joy quietly waiting in the wings of my chaotic evening. I acknowledged its sweetness as well as heaven's divine goodness.

"God works in mysterious ways. Those wind gusts that kicked up are the only reason the festival shut down earlier than usual." I sipped tea and looked at Greenie, recalling how the night breeze had increased to such a strong degree that items were mercilessly blown about and even a table toppled over. A sudden sprinkle of rain had added to the unpleasant conditions, resulting in the festival's premature ending. "But did you notice how the wind lessened and the rain was barely a drizzle when we reached my place?"

"Girl, God sent wind and rain and shut the festival down just so we could see the wide behind of Willard Brinks?" Greenie grimaced. "That's one sighting I didn't need."

"At least I finally saw him naked." I voiced that without thinking.

"What does that mean?"

The kitchen phone rang, sparing me from having to respond.

"Who in the world is calling here this time of night?" Greenie pushed away from the table, intending to head for the ringing apparatus.

"It's my mother. Don't answer." I continued as she looked at me questioningly. "I know Willard. He's probably filled her ears with all kinds of foolishness...except his being in an outhouse acting like a possum in heat."

"Precisely." Greenie repositioned herself at the table. "So... back to what you were saying...about finally seeing him naked."

I took a calming sip of tea before quietly reiterating the ridiculousness of my sad, pitiful marriage. The constant criticisms. Twice-weekly scheduling of non-intimate intimacy. Willard's puritanical ideations that prohibited my enjoyment. And his collection of pornographic postcards beneath the bathroom sink.

"He made space for them, but never for me."

Greenie's eyes teared up and she grasped my good hand as I spoke, but she waited until I finished before uttering a sound. "Oh, LoLo..."

"I don't need pity, Greenie! I never wanted any of this, but I allowed it. So I take responsibility for accepting what I shouldn't have...starting with Willard's fat hand in marriage. *Oh Jesus, Greenie!*"

I pitched forward, body shaking, breathing heavily.

She jumped from her seat. *"What is it?"*

I broke out in a sweat and felt cold, clammy. My hands flailed wildly. "I need paper! Pencil. Something."

I struggled to breathe as she raced from the kitchen only to swiftly return moments later with implements that she thrust into my waiting grasp.

My eyes watered and my chest heaved as I bent over the table, furiously drawing.

Greenie silently stood, looking over my shoulder watching every stroke I made. Yet, it was as if I was alone with my muse, lost in a swirling vortex.

Tears blurred my vision as I surrendered to an overwhelming need flowing through my being to create that which didn't previously exist as if God flowed through my fingertips.

When finished I sagged in my chair, exhausted, and dropped the drawing implement Greenie had given me atop the table only to realize it was a tube of lipstick.

"My. Dear. Jesus." Greenie's voice was breathless. "LoLo, what just happened?"

I said nothing and simply shook my head, feeling as if I'd been possessed. Only once before had I had such an experience: when Gabe was shot in the war and lost his arm on the battlefield.

Closing my eyes, I caught my breath before looking at the paper in front of me, expecting another grotesque caricature of Willard. Instead, in the soothing, earthy hues of Greenie's brown lipstick, emerged a being who was more spirit than woman.

"She's beautiful." Greenie's voice was awestruck. "Who is she?"

"I'm not sure, but I need to show it to Flo. I think it's Lady Liberty."

"Lady Liberty?" Greenie took an involuntary step backward. "How could you draw her without even knowing what she looks like? And why?"

"I've no idea other than...I think I've heard her...I mean," I quickly amended when her eyes grew big. "I may have felt her presence lately."

She stared at me for a few seconds before quietly exhaling. "Well...according to legend she *is* an emancipator who comes for those in need. Maybe she's here to help you get free."

"Partially." I studied the rendering of the beautiful presence draped in loose, flowing clothing with a multi-patterned headwrap situated as if her crown. "I feel like...and don't ask me how I know this...but what I feel she wants me to know is that the only one who can rescue me from all the things I don't want to live or be...is me."

Nineteen

I am the one to rescue me from what I don't want to live or be.

A condensed version of the message from Mama Liberty floated through my mind like autumn leaves on a soft breeze as I lay next to Greenie unable to sleep. My dear one found it too disturbing to continue using the bedroom she'd shared with Conroy and hadn't slept there since her husband's passing. The spare room had become her domain, yet she'd offered it to me without a second thought.

I can't kick you out and put you on the sofa, Greenie. This bed's big enough for the two of us. We can huddle up like we did when we were kids having sleepovers.

Her lack of protest was proof that she craved human contact as much as I did. After baths and a bowl of banana pudding, we'd bundled together in bed with the innocence of children.

Now, wide awake as my precious friend slept, I stared at the ceiling, acknowledging how starved I was for love and affection after enduring a marriage that offered little besides deprivation. Mentally, emotionally, and physically—each area of my union with Willard had suffered deficits that I could finally admit were nothing less than abusive. While the man I married had never outright hit me, his treatment overflowed with a cruelty designed to make me feel incomplete.

Was there ever a time when he was consistently kind?

Certainly, in the beginning, when were college colleagues. And even after "I do", particularly when he needed or wanted something. Somewhere along the way he'd removed his mask, revealing his true colors, his true face. Neither was acceptable nor wanted. For the sake of my own health and wellness, I chose to release the toxic thing we'd erroneously dubbed a marriage. I chose to move beyond and live.

I turned toward Greenie when she mumbled something in her sleep. If my ears weren't playing tricks, she'd whispered Conroy's name.

I smoothed a curl from her forehead, my heart aching knowing how deeply she still loved and missed her husband.

I can't imagine how difficult it is for you to live without your beloved.

That thought faded away as I realized I *could* imagine living life in such fashion only because I'd lived without Gabe.

I am the one to rescue me from what I don't want to live or be.

I latched onto my earlier mantra in an effort to silence thoughts of Gabriel. Not in an act of avoidance. But to keep my mind clear. I had decisions to make, and things to consider. But one thing was certain: I would be contacting Otis Richelieu, Colemanville's lawyer.

There was no need for pretense. Willard Brinks and I were finished.

I inhaled deeply, thankful for the peace-filled environment surrounding me.

The countryside of Colemanville had fewer human inhabitants, allowing the glory of nature to have preeminence. Out here at Greenie's farm there were no noisy neighbors, cars backfiring, or the normal sounds of a neighborhood. Here cicadas and bullfrogs harmonized with the wind and the patter of rain that drizzled on and off again. The sweet symphony didn't lull me to sleep. It energized my being and pulled me toward a calm, sweet sensation that made me think of Gabe once again.

The honey color of his eyes. The gentleness of his lips. The broad kindness of his spirit. His humor and strength.

I forced my mind away only for my thoughts to ricochet back to the flesh I'd earlier witnessed on display.

Lord, was Willard really having relations in the outhouse with Pumpkin?

I shook my head and exhaled into the night, still stunned by the sight of the two of them going at it like rabid rabbits.

An image of Willard and Pumpkin foaming at the mouth and copulating as Doc Everett injected rabies vaccines into their naked backsides filled my mind and left me laughing.

I clamped a hand over my mouth when Greenie mumbled again, this time something about the sunflowers she planned to plant next spring.

Gabe loves polly seeds.

It was late, but clearly I needed to occupy my mind and my time to keep my thoughts from orbiting around the one I'd hurt and who'd hurt me as well.

Think about your upcoming trip to Raleigh.

Visions of standing before The Nubian-Kush committee in a few days and presenting myself as the best candidate for the senior artist fellowship lasted long enough to put an anxious smile on my face before my wayward mind did as it pleased and flowed back to Gabe.

Exhaling irritably, I pushed back the quilt and quietly eased from bed. I slipped my borrowed robe over my equally borrowed nightwear and padded toward the door, hoping another cup of chamomile would help me fall asleep.

"LoLo...my keys are on the table."

I turned toward Greenie, thinking she was mumbling in her sleep, but she continued drowsily.

"Ain't nothing easy about living without the one your heart wants."

Her words were soft enough to be lost beneath the sounds of the country night with its insect chorus and light rain, yet I heard every one. "Greenie, what're you going on about?"

"Conroy ain't here. Gabe is. Y'all need to talk while you still can."

She turned in the opposite direction, pulled the quilt up to her neck, and resumed sleeping, breathing in a way she'd never admit to be snoring.

I studied her darkened silhouette before exiting the room and closing the door behind me. Slipping on my coat and shoes, I headed for the kitchen. And the keys.

I DIDN'T DRIVE SLOWLY, didn't use the time for thinking, preparing, or reflecting. I hurried toward town with a sense of urgency, determined not to run away from doing what was necessary. I turned onto the Thurmans' street and approached their house only to be suddenly guided by a pressing inkling. Looking at the Thurmans' darkened home, I had the sense that Gabe wasn't there, and chose to follow my intuition. Driving slowly to prevent Old Faithful's noisy engine from disturbing the slumbering neighborhood, I eased down the street until reaching the outlet that opened onto the road that led me to where I hoped to find him and sped away in that direction.

"Come on, girl, you can do this!" I wasn't sure if I was coaxing Old Faithful or myself as Greenie's old truck coughed and wheezed, protesting being driven at a higher speed than customary. She rattled as we rolled, still I refused to let up until arriving on Fig Street where darkened buildings huddled together like slumbering giants against the drizzle that was now full-fledged rain.

The windshield wipers worked overtime, their scraping hum the only sound in the night as I eased Old Faithful down the narrow back alley, halting midway. My heart raced as I hopped from the truck and dashed toward the rear door of the building. I raised a hand but the door slammed inward before I could knock.

"Dammit, Ilona, I could've blown your head off!"

I stared at the moonlit barrel of Gabe's rifle, momentarily frozen by shock.

"What the hell are you doing? Why're you driving around in the rain at some unholy hour in the black of morning?"

I stepped toward him, shaking my head to fling off paralysis. I moved forward cautiously, pushing aside the barrel of the rifle still aimed in my direction.

His hold was fierce as if he was digesting the fact that it was me and not someone intending harm or malfeasance. Even in moonlight his piercing, unwavering glare was evident, and I imagined it replicated the expressions he'd worn on the battlefield.

"It's okay, Gabe. I promise."

His grip lessened the slightest bit. It was enough for me to slowly but successfully remove the rifle from his hold. Carefully, I leaned forward, placing it inside the room, against the storeroom wall. I straightened my posture, intending to step back, only to find Gabe and I chest-to-chest.

"Why're you here, Ilona Ann? Go home to your husband."

His voice was a deep rumble that penetrated my skin and rolled from my heart to my feet. I was instantly warm despite the rain as I looked up at him. Truth formed on my lips, that I was there to confront him, to have my say and allow him to have his. And, as far as I was concerned, there was no husband.

I kissed him instead.

Wrapping my arms about his neck, I pressed forward, causing him to stumble backward into the storeroom. He anchored his arm about me. Perhaps for balance. Perhaps in intimacy. I didn't care right then. Kicking the door shut behind me, my only clear thought was that I craved and needed him.

"I love you, Gabe."

I whispered my truth against his lips while holding him tighter, deepening our kiss.

Whatever his reservations may have been, they vaporized and vanished.

A burning sensation sped through me as he pushed my coat from my body and held me tightly, lavishing love on me in ways that only amplified my greed. A strangled moan escaped my lips as his mouth left mine to lance my shoulders, my neck, with the heat of his tongue. When his hand strayed to my breast, I gasped and held onto him, feeling as if I might fall only for Gabe to lift me with his powerful left arm.

Embracing his neck, I wrapped my legs around his waist, trusting he knew his way in the dark as he backed up until reaching the cot. He sat with me on his lap facing him, my thighs still tightly clutching his waist as if I never wanted to be separated.

I ached to be as close to him as his own skin.

Greenie's nightgown was a sudden hindrance. Lifting it overhead, I carelessly discarded it, preferring the rough texture of Gabe's palm as he tenderly caressed my breasts. Closing my eyes, I savored his touch and every thrill it created only to lose my breath when his mouth took over the luscious torment his hand began.

My back curved inward. Moans filled the air—mine and his—indicating shared pleasure as giver and recipient. The more he kissed, licked, and drew me into the warm well of his mouth, the more deliciously wanton I felt and the more I wanted to receive. But I also longed to give. Lifting onto my knees, I wriggled out of my underwear before managing to ease Gabe's pants down his legs, his shirt over his head, leaving us both wonderfully naked.

In the dark my hands were my guides, gliding over his skin, making a decadent acquaintance. His broad shoulders. His firm back. The hard strength of his biceps. I felt full of the sweetest of colors, as if floating in bliss as I ran my hands over Gabe's form in my quest to prove this was real. As he gently sucked the tender places on my neck, causing warmth to pool between my legs, my fingers explored the majesty of him.

My hands slowly slid down his arms only to pause when he stiffened the slightest bit as my fingers neared the space where his right forearm no longer existed.

"You're whole and beautiful, Gabriel Thurman. Nothing is missing." I sealed that whispered truth with deep, endless kisses, branding him for myself as we explored each other until we were breathless and aching for complete union. Still facing him, I repositioned myself, lifting on my knees, and slowly received him.

Overcome by sensation as I lowered myself onto his solidity, I buried my face in his neck, thrilled by our oneness.

Safety waited in his embrace as we kissed. There was no censure, only acceptance, as our hips, our bodies, moved in precious unison as if possessed by a color-filled whirlwind that rose higher and wider until I shattered beyond recognition.

The sounds and sensations of my completion were foreign and overwhelming as Gabe laid me on the cot and thrust deeper still, my legs wrapped tightly about him until he too shattered in our watercolor whirlwind.

Twenty

A ballet of shadows and light danced across my skin in the soft glow of a small lantern. The golden glow illuminated every place he touched with sweet tenderness as we lay intertwined in purest bliss. His touch was gentle, yet stimulating, leaving ribbons of warmth on my skin. My body tingled. Peace filled me. I snuggled against his chest, praying I'd never be forced to leave the wonders of this sanctuary where the air smelled of fresh wood and oils that caused his craftsmanship to gleam. Those smells were now a part of me and would forever be attached to poignant memories of our loving.

"How's your arm? Does it still hurt?"

The deep resonance of his voice drew me away from the serene slumber to which my body and soul wanted to surrender after experiencing immaculate ecstasy. Forcing myself away from sleep, I yawned and stretched like a milk-fed cat, barely glancing at the small area I'd injured last week that he now lovingly traced with his forefinger.

Quietly, I laughed. "I only flew off a bike, could've cracked my head open, and was almost run over by a wild man driving Big Blue. But it's fine. Thank you."

He chuckled softly. "I'm innocent. I was distracted by your pretty, round backside on that bike seat so blame yourself. Not me."

"Oh, hush and quit talking dirty."

"Baby, you won't know dirty talk 'til you been in the field with a platoon of men."

"I dare not imagine. But may I ask the same question... about *your* arm?" I looked up at him. "How do *you* feel?"

He studied my face a moment before focusing on the ceiling where lantern light frolicked. "My feelings now ain't nowhere near how I felt then...when it first happened. I've had time to come to understand that this is who and how I am now." He raised what remained of his right arm. "That don't mean at times it still ain't an adjustment."

I forced myself not to press for more when he lapsed into silence.

"Sometimes I get an itch, go to scratch, and nothing's there. I've learned to live with that."

I let his words settle in me before quietly asking, "How did it happen...exactly?"

He pushed a strand of hair away from my face and kissed my forehead. "I'm not fixin' to fill this pretty head with gory stories of—"

"Don't treat me like a porcelain doll. If I asked, that means I want to know."

"For what reason?"

"Because I love you and it was something extremely impactful that you experienced, Gabe. Regardless if *you* think I can handle it or not, I won't break."

I returned his firm stare, unwilling to acquiesce.

"Sweet Rivers, I swear you must've been born stubborn." He exhaled loudly and held me tighter, cradling me in the crook of his arm as if anchoring us both through a recounting of the most life-altering part of his personal history.

"I told you in my letters so you already know I was assigned to the 761st over in Louisiana under Lieutenant Colonel Paul Bates. That was one tough man who didn't take B.S. from nobody. Still, I gotta say he was pretty fair. All things considered."

Training was intense, but so was war. By the time The 761st Tank Battalion departed for Europe they were a well-oiled unit ready to serve as allies in a fight for freedom.

"They pumped us up with all kinds of speeches, but you could tell our commanders didn't fully believe in us or our ability to help the French."

The 761st Tank Battalion was comprised of Negro soldiers. It was segregated.

President Truman integrated the military last year in 1948 whereas the 761st, or The Black Panthers as they named themselves, was formed in 1942, a year prior to Gabe's enlistment. When Gabe, as a member of The Black Panthers, arrived in France in October in 1944, I was in my final year in college.

I traced the panther tattoo on his right bicep. "I was being rebellious and painting instead of studying English while you were risking your life on a daily basis."

He shrugged. "No two battlefields look the same, but we're all fighting for something." His tone brightened suddenly. "Hey, you know that Jack Robinson that got signed to the Dodgers? That cat was one of the Panthers! But he never saw action."

"Really! Because?"

"Young blood refused to sit at the back of a military bus during training at Fort Hood and got court-martialed. Guess it was a blessing in disguise. He wouldn't be running bases and breaking racial lines if he'd gone to Europe and lost a limb. Or his life."

I made a sound of acknowledgement, appreciative but not fully invested right then in another man's journey when what I needed was for him to trust me with his story.

He fell quiet before inhaling deeply, as if finally he too was ready.

"The Panthers took the town of Morville-les-Vic back for the French before pushing toward Germany." His voice was low. Heavy. "We were led by Captain John D. Long of B Company, a Colored officer. And, man, was *he* something! Mean as hell, but I guess under the circumstances he had to be. We were supporting our 26th Infantry Division and those kraut bastards had anti-tank artillery. That didn't stop us from coming."

They were under heavy fire when a Sherman tank ahead of Gabe's exploded mere seconds after being hit, after two crew members managed to escape an initial fusillade.

"When I saw them bleeding on that road, I didn't stop to think. I was a gunner, but I left my tank position tryna get to them."

Seconds after abandoning his own tank, it was struck by enemy fire and essentially incinerated.

"My whole crew was gone." He snapped his fingers. "Like that! They gave their lives. I didn't do nothing but catch a bullet and shrapnel."

My head on his chest, listening to his heartbeat, I felt the anger coursing through him and warming his flesh. I raised up a bit to look at him. "I'm so sorry to hear about the loss of your fellow tank crew...but it almost sounds like you wished you'd died with them."

His jaw twitched as he ground his teeth before slowly exhaling. "I don't remember much from the time I was hit 'til waking up in the hospital like this." He raised his amputated limb. "But, yeah, I wished I was dead back then. And it wasn't just because of physical pain, but the soldiers I tried to help didn't get my help at all. And my crew was gone..."

Quietly, he spoke the names of his fallen comrades as if an homage.

"They were good men."

"As are you, Gabriel Aloysius Thurman. Your sacrifice didn't cost you your life, but you did sacrifice. Your bravery isn't something to sneeze at. You gave your best and I couldn't be more proud of you." I sat up, pulling the quilt to cover my nakedness. "Even if you didn't come back to Colemanville after your discharge and completing rehabilitation, you're still a damn good man. And why is that?"

"You asking why I skipped out on Colemanville?"

My unflinching stare was my only response.

The cot shifted as he sat up and rested his wide back against the wall with me. "Because you deserved better, baby."

"Well that's not what I got by any stretch of the imagination! And staying with you or not should've been *my* decision to make, not yours. You and your bullheaded pride took that choice away."

He nodded. "I suppose we did. Forgive me. That was unfair."

I sat with his apology, accepting it before giving into curiosity. "Where did you go? What did you do after rehabilitation?"

He rested his hand on my thigh, his fingers doodling over my skin. "Some of this, that, and the third. You know that restlessness that used to nip at me every now and again? Yeah...well...I let it have at it." He followed wanderlust up the eastern seaboard as far as Maine, working odd jobs and lodging at Colored hotels or boarding houses when available. "I stayed in Harlem for a good spell and wouldn't mind going back there. Wouldn't mind going back to Europe either, specifically France. Those Frenchies honored our war efforts and treated us like equals. Like men. That's one reason why I didn't come home, Sweet Rivers, because I didn't just feel like less than a man. I felt less than human."

The emotional, psychological impact of his injury left a crushing pain on my chest. My soul ached knowing he'd endured such traumatic devastation. Yet, the part of my heart that had been ravaged by his absence and rejection flared into action. I wanted to take him to task and defend myself. My love was substantive, not fickle. I wasn't a coward or so shallow as to have turned away from us in disgust.

Even so, I told myself this was *his* experience, and something I'd never lived through or with. He'd handled matters as he was able and in ways he thought were best.

I chose to accept that. I couldn't pass judgment.

"I wasn't ready to face you like this." He cleared his throat, declining the tears that welled up. "I needed time to get my head straight. Working hard during the day helped block out memories. Nights were ruthless. I couldn't sleep thinking about you and what I was missing and took to walking around towns like a gotdamn phantom. When walking didn't work, I drank like a fish until winding up in a Catholic church dark-thirty one morning, puking my guts all over the altar and crying like a big ass baby."

He chuckled briefly.

"I don't know where the priest was or why candles were lit that time of morning, but I looked up at Jesus and he looked back at me. I was like, 'Come on, Lord, you gonna help me?' Jesus said, 'Ey, man, you see they got me up here with nails in my hands and feet? Get your big rusty butt up and help your damn self'."

I couldn't help giggling. "Stop lying on the Lord, Gabriel."

"Father, forgive me. But seriously..." He played with the stubble on his jaw and looked at the far wall. "Lying in vomit and looking up at that life size crucifix thinking Jesus managed walking around with holes in his hands and feet kinda sobered me. I cleaned up my mess and staggered out of there thinking wasn't nothing left for me to do but accept this thing and get on with living."

He stopped studying the wall and looked at me.

"Took a minute to get myself all the way together and work up the courage to bring my ass back here. It took Mama's letter to do it. I hopped the next thing smoking, but even that was too late for grace. I was pissed to the point of crazy and knew if I got off that train the day you were engaged I woulda killed—"

"What do you mean if you got off the train the day I was engaged?"

I listened, horrified by his account of receiving a letter from his mother informing him that "some nerdy, four-eyed man was sniffing around me", and she had it on good record that he intended to propose. That man would have been Willard, but how Miz Thurman knew of an intended proposal was a mystery.

Mother told Miz Grayson!

I questioned how my mother had known in advance only to recall that I lived in an era when men asked a woman's father for her hand in marriage. Still, something didn't sit right with me and my mind sped forward, swiftly painting a likely scenario and conclusion.

My mother was loquacious, as was the mercantile's owner, and she must have shared the news, perhaps during one of their sewing circles.

Mother had banked on Miz Grayson's rushing to tell her closest friend, Miz Thurman who, in turn, would have notified Gabriel. And she most definitely did. If I'd surmised correctly, then the whole thing was devious, my parents' way of ensuring my beloved knew the door had firmly closed on our romance. In my heart of hearts I knew it was intentional. Not accidental.

It was their way of guaranteeing that he'd stay away.

I closed my eyes and took calming breaths, refusing to shed one tear over their deviousness.

"I was here, Sweet Rivers. I saw you. Your family. And *him* at the station. But for all of our sake I stayed on that train."

"Gabe, you can't be serious..."

"You were wearing that blue dress with the black lace overlay that I loved seeing you in. And that crystal hummingbird brooch I gave you before I left for basic training. He gave you some sorry looking bouquet of half-dead daisies. You seemed less than yourself, but your family was cheering, celebrating the engagement."

Stunned, I repositioned myself so we were face-to-face. "But I never saw you!"

"Mr. Robertson did."

My mouth hung open.

He nodded. "I was stalking down that train car aisle ready to jump off and stuff my foot in Brinks' unmentionables. But your father saw me coming." His voice seemingly plummeted off a cliff and into a dark hole as he finished. "You remember Mr. Robertson grabbing Brinks and walking him around the station platform, cheering?"

"Yes..."

"And how Mr. Robertson kept raising that fool's arms like he'd survived ten rounds with Joe Louis?"

Even then I'd thought it strange behavior for my typically reserved father, an unnecessary celebration. In an exaggerated fashion he'd lifted, fanned, and waved Willard's arms all over the place as if declaring him a prize champion, congratulating him over and again on our engagement and calling him his fine, healthy son with the strength of God in his arms.

"He was sending messages, letting me know I couldn't

compete with Brinks as an amputee. It was simple battle tactics, but he got his point across. It knocked the wind out of me. Left me thinking he was right and I was ruined. So I did the only thing that made sense. I took a seat and rode that train not caring where it went. Anywhere was better than watching you marry another man."

That's why Father asked me to forgive him!

It seemed bizarre yet inconsequential back then, his gesturing with Willard as if a puppet master, when all along it was heartlessness in action.

I couldn't keep the tears from rolling down my face or my voice from choking. "But Willard got on that train…"

"Yeah. He did." He wiped at my tears. "Grinning like a damn fool on Christmas. Took everything in me not to toss him outta window once we got rolling. But I decided then and there that it was my last trip to Colemanville."

"But you came back for Budd…after his cardiac arrest."

"Yeah, I came back for my brother, and to help my family. Partially. But the bigger picture is I came home because I was tired of running away from what I couldn't have. Not having *you*, not the lack of this arm, is why I stayed away from Colemanville."

I placed a hand on my heart, wishing I could undo the hurtful past. Unable to, I pressed my forehead against his and wrapped my arms about him.

Together we wept.

Twenty-One

I never meant to stay. Or to fall asleep against his chest and be awakened hours later by the hunger of his warm touch on my flesh. Yet, I would trade the world for the experience of loving him again. My love's embrace was heaven on earth, an inescapable invitation to share ourselves once again until we rocketed, tumbled into explosive brilliance that rendered us weak, breathless. Our love, physically expressed, fed my soul and painted my spirit, leaving me unwilling to do without it.

"I have to go." My words were a whisper against his eyelids, his jaw, his chin as I kissed his smooth skin in the aftermath of repeat oneness. "Greenie's probably wondering what happened to me."

"Greenie's a grown woman. She *knows*. She ain't wondering."

I laughed and buried my face in his neck. "I feel scandalous."

"Comes with the territory of driving around nude at night."

I pushed onto my elbow and stared at him. "I did no such thing!"

"Didn't take much for us to get you out of what little you had on, so you might as well have been. Trust me, Sweet Rivers, I ain't complaining." He nuzzled my neck, kissing sensitive places in a slow, thorough way that left me barely able to think and on the verge of reconsidering my need to leave.

"I have to go, Gabe. It's late." My words came out slow, lazy.

"You mean it's early. It's near 'bout morning."

Neither of us made an effort to release the other despite the encroaching dawn. I didn't resist his hand trailing slowly up and down my thighs, leaving electrical currents along my flesh, until his hand settled between my legs as his mouth claimed my breast. Pleasure curled and danced through my being as a ragged moan escaped my lips, as I arched into him wanting more of the pleasures we'd already experienced. I opened myself, welcoming another journey toward satiation even as strange yet oddly familiar sounds in the distance wormed their way into my sensation-soaked consciousness.

Only Gabe's sudden tension yanked me fully from our path toward satisfaction. Snatching his discarded pants from the floor, he hurried into them as the sounds outdoors grew louder, strident and intense.

"Don't move. Stay here." His fierce whisper seemed even more ominous as he doused the lantern light and eased noiselessly through the dark storeroom until I could no longer feel his presence.

Unable to trace his movements, I sat up, imagining his stealth would have been invaluable on any battlefield. Yet, I was unable to fully appreciate his skill as the noise outdoors increased. Voices in the alleyway beyond the walls of the storeroom made my breath catch as the sound of a gun cocking was instantly followed by the door being flung open.

My heart hammered wildly in my chest as he stepped outside, pistol aimed at the ready.

Screams filled the air, upsetting the dawn's red, orange, and amber glory.

"Gabe, don't!"

His holding the pistol steady on whatever he'd targeted was proof my screamed caution had little impact. By the light floating through the doorway I located Greenie's nightgown and scrambled into it before tumbling from the room into a cacophony of outrage and fear.

I stared in disbelief at my three oldest sisters cowering and caterwauling near the rear of Father's Pontiac. With Willard.

A thick gauze bandage covered his nose as he stood raging into the new day as if he alone bore the wounds of our failed relationship. "See! It's exactly as I said. I married a ravenous whore and strumpet!"

I grabbed Gabe about the waist when he lunged forward in response to Willard's raving accusation, realizing all the while the pistol had been aimed at only him. "Lower the gun, Gabe. Please."

He did so slowly, reluctantly, but his focus never wavered. His gaze alone was enough to bore a hole into Willard.

"Ilona, how could you?" Clearly my holding Gabe in place granted my oldest sister Theodora the courage to speak. "You're a disgrace!"

Viola added her outrage. "How dare you sully our family name by laying up with..." She waved toward Gabe as if at a loss for words..."someone other than your husband!"

"We weren't raised in such a moralless way. Mother and Father will be devastated." Theodora broke into sobs and nearly collapsed in Viola's arms.

Only Olivia stood looking from me to Gabe and back again as if, perhaps, she'd be willing to understand that what she saw was purer than anything I'd ever shared with the man standing beside her, fists clenched as if battle-ready.

I watched Willard watching me, his expression somehow wounded yet triumphant. "Your fine, upstanding sisters now serve as witnesses to the nature of your flagrant and abhorrent behavior."

"You're as bad as Ravena."

"What does Ravena have to do with anything?" Ignoring Willard and his hypocritical opinion, I stared at Viola, wondering why she was invoking our one sister who lived beyond Colemanville.

Theodora composed herself and glared at me. "You and Ravena have earned yourselves a place in hell. Enjoy each other's company."

She slid onto the backseat of our parents' Pontiac, openly weeping and aided by Viola as if my moral failures reduced her to incapacitation.

"She's a shameless spectacle!" Willard turned to Olivia, the only one who hadn't yet pronounced me a degenerate. "Look at her. She's nearly naked. She should be marched through town like Hester Prynne with a scarlet letter seared into her forehead."

I released Gabe, descended the steps, ignoring his calling me back to the safety of him. I stopped mere inches from Willard and stared hard at the foolery who'd failed as a husband, marveling that I'd ever felt so hopeless as to have accepted him.

Bending down, I scooped up a handful of gravel and offered it. "Throw the first stone if you're sinless."

He lurched backward in a display of offense before turning toward my sisters, high on the scent of his own arrogance. "I've never been so disrespected! And I refuse to tolerate it. Particularly in front of a one-arm, whoremongering monstrosity like Thurman."

I acted on instinct, flinging that handful of gravel at him. "Two arms haven't made you moral or fully human!"

My sisters gasped as Willard stood there bug-eyed, mouth open wide enough to catch flies. But only momentarily. Sputtering and spewing obscenities into the dawn, he grabbed me in an attempt to force me into the car. My resistance caused his increased efforts, his jerking me so violently that we both fell, landing on my left shoulder in a way that shot fiery pain throughout my being.

My agonized scream was swallowed beneath a thunderous blast splitting the morning in half.

Willard immediately rolled away from me, shaking in terror at the bullet that had whizzed over his head, barely missing him. He shuddered and cowered on the ground as Gabe stalked toward him, rifle smoking and steady.

He stood over Willard, pressing the end of that rifle into my husband's belly—voice low, intense, and gritty. "Touch her *ever* again and I promise you'll never see or touch another woman."

Gritting my teeth against the pain racking my shoulder, I accepted Gabe's assisting me to my feet before he retrained that rifle on Willard. "You okay, Sweet Rivers?"

I assured him I was despite the burning agony in my left shoulder. "Gabriel." Needing to keep the man I loved from winding up in a jail cell, I slowly pushed the rifle off-target until feeling his tension ebb a bit. "Please...let me have it."

He stopped glaring at the man cowering on the ground to look at me, his jaw grinding and twitching.

Quietly repeating my request, I waited until he slowly stepped away without relinquishing his rifle, maintaining his focus on Willard.

"Take your sorry ass out of here, Brinks." He turned and headed for the rear door of Thurman's Fine Furniture, tossing over his shoulder as he went, "And seeing as how you're one of those slow-learning, half-a-sack-of-a-man men, lemme repeat myself for your benefit." He paused in the doorway without bothering to look back. "Touch her again and you'll figure out with your last breath that I shot and missed on purpose. I won't miss again."

I breathed in relief when Gabe disappeared indoors before turning and considering the frozen tableau before me.

Theodora and Viola clung to each other in the rear seat as Olivia leaned against the Pontiac in a state of paralysis. I offered them reassurance that everything was okay before pivoting my attention to Willard. He lay quivering on the ground, fluid darkening his crotch and seeping down his pant leg.

I wanted to feel embarrassed for him and the odor of his urine sharpening the cool autumn air except I felt nothing toward him and never would again. "You came here for no other reason than to shame me. You shamed yourself instead."

"I'm only here to bring you back home." Fear had Willard's voice trembling uncontrollably. "To the safety of your family. And to spare you your sins."

"And what of your nude pictures, spousal neglect, and sexual exchange in the outhouse with Pumpkin?"

He struggled to push himself upright at the sound of my sisters' sharp inhalations.

I continued, disinterested in anyone's understanding or approval. "I could care less about offering excuses or justifications, but I didn't come here in retaliation or to spite you, Willard. I choose to be here because I know what love is and isn't. I can't live with our bastardized version."

"Your conduct as a wife is worthy of damnation."

"If I wind up in hell, like Theodora said, we'll keep each other company." I turned and headed toward the rear steps.

"Ilona?"

Despite the searing pain in my shoulder, I paused at Olivia's approach.

"I can only speak for myself, but I'm not here to shame you. I came because Mother was worried when no one answered at Greenie's. Last night or this morning. We drove out there afraid something horrible had happened."

"And you knew to come here because?"

She ducked her head and cleared her throat before facing me again. "Because Jonathan and Budd Jr. are best friends. I remembered overhearing Budd Jr. telling Jonathan his Uncle Gabe sometimes slept at the family business."

My nephew, Jonathan, wasn't to blame, and I was too tired to fault my sister and this army of moralists for some misguided confrontation. I simply grimaced at the pain that radiated through my throbbing shoulder when she hugged me. Stepping out of her embrace, I resumed my journey to the back steps.

Glancing up, I found Gabe reaching out to aid my ascent. Gently, he embraced me with the sound of the Pontiac's departure fading behind us.

His voice was a dangerous rumble against my cheek as I rested my head against the comfort of his chest. "We need to get you to Doc Everett."

Twenty-Two

I was late to the schoolhouse that day despite Gabe making the ten-mile drive to Jacksonville like a bat freed from Hades.

"It's only my shoulder, Gabe. I'm not having a baby."

He glanced at me, not a stitch of humor on his face, insides still tightly coiled over the manner in which my injury had been sustained. He'd cursed Willard ten ways to Sunday and had relented hunting him down like "a rabid, mangy mutt" only after I'd threatened to turn him into Sheriff Weaver if he did.

Our love might've been illicit to some, but I refused to have blood on it.

Despite his chaotic relationship with Floretta, Doc Everett, a consummate healer and caring physician, met us at his clinic just as the sun breached the horizon. He exhaled with relief when announcing my shoulder wasn't broken, but severely sprained and impaired. "Looks like some bruising is already forming. I want you in this sling for the next two weeks to isolate any movement. No strenuous activity. No heavy lifting."

He provided a small bottle of pain medication with instructions that I was to phone him immediately if anything worsened. Particularly if there was fever or swelling. He escorted us to Big Blue, hugging me carefully and shaking Gabe's hand, without questioning our being there together. Without passing judgment.

The ride home was less tense. Despite Gabe's insisting I not drive Old Faithful while wearing a sling, I refused to be treated like an invalid and drove myself back to Greenie's after kissing him deeply, regretting nothing. Not our love or its intimacy. I drove away, periodically glancing at him in the rearview mirror until his magnificence was a mere desirable memory in the distance.

I tried not to relive our lovemaking as I headed toward Greenie's only to find my mind and body trapped by the exquisiteness I'd experienced. The heat. The thrill. Every overwhelming sensation.

I've never not loved you since the first time we kissed, Sweet Rivers.

His expressed sentiment caressed my soul, leaving me overflowing with lush decadence.

My thoughts were so consumed with Gabe that I found myself turning onto my street out of habit instead of being on the right road to my best friend's.

"Might as well stop and grab a few of my things."

I wasn't sure how long I'd stay with Greenie, but considered it best to have the basics on hand as I parked in front of my parents' and started up the walkway only to pause at the sight of my luggage waiting on the front porch like abandoned children. Whether Willard or Mother was responsible made no difference. The screen door was locked, preventing my entry.

One by one, I lugged my suitcases to the back of Old

Faithful, knowing I'd been banned. For them, I *was* Hester Prynne.

The hot bath and breakfast of fried eggs, scrapple, and flapjacks waiting on me at Greenie's helped mellow my jagged edges. I felt restored, relieved, and strangely giddy by the time the meal was finished.

"Girl, after all the foolery you endured today, why're you grinning?" She shook her head, as if still reeling from what I'd recounted for her benefit.

My smile broadened as I looked at my dearest friend seated on the opposite side of the table. "Honey, I finally had some good fuss and ruckus."

IGNORING Gabe and Greenie's advice to stay home and rest my shoulder, I went to my Tuesday morning art class, albeit a few minutes late. My precious kindergartners were happy to see me, waving and calling out greetings as I entered the room, apologizing to their teacher for my late appearance.

"What happened, Miz R.B.? Why're you wearing that thing?"

Willard Brinks fell on me.

I provided my curious kindergartners a safer rendition of facts before moving into our new Thanksgiving project. Turkeys. Pumpkins. Pilgrim hats and Indian headpieces. We spent the morning happily planning the month ahead that would be filled with painting, drawing, coloring and constructing. When they were dismissed at their usual time midday, I went on lunch break slightly tired yet stimulated. And unable to stop thinking of Gabe.

My shoulder throbbed relentlessly. As did the gateway to paradise between my legs. I walked about the schoolyard hoping the autumn chill would lower my internal temperature and restore my decency.

Honey, you left that on that cot at Thurman's Fine Furniture.

Laughing at my lusciously degenerate state, I turned toward the schoolhouse as Principal North clanged the cowbell he faithfully used to signal the end of recess or meal breaks. I approached my first and second graders where they lined up, hands clasped in front of them, quietly at attention.

"Don't you look like perfect little artists!" I smiled proudly and quickly explained why my arm was in a sling to avoid countless questions. "Today is the first day of a month of Thanksgiving. Is everyone ready to enjoy a colorful day?"

"Yes, ma'am!"

I led the way, realizing it was Tuesday but there would be no obligatory relations. No scheduled intimacy between Willard and me. Not that night or ever again. My whole soul skipped joyfully as I proceeded into the building, ready to share creative time with the beautiful little beings walking quietly behind me.

"Please sit in a semi-circle around my easel so we can plan this month's creations." I never came to school without planning lessons in advance, but I also loved fostering little ones' creativity and their sense of empowerment. Most were naturally curious and uninhibited at this age, but being receptive to their input also enhanced their openness and made art less intimidating.

I stood aside, watching as they entered single-file, feeling as if my joy of sharing art had somehow increased overnight.

That's a side effect of good fuss and ruckus.

My face warmed with embarrassment and I wanted to laugh until I noticed Callie as she entered at the end of the line.

My niece was subdued, absent of her usual effervescent energy.

"Callandra...what's wrong, sweetie?"

She shook her head and avoided eye contact as she hurried past me to sit as instructed. I studied her, seeing what looked like a dried trail of tears marking her face. My brows furrowed as she lowered herself onto the rug in an odd way. I was instantly alarmed, wondering if something had happened at recess.

"Miz R.B.?" My attention was averted by Packer's little Peanut sitting cross-legged, hand in the air.

"Yes, Packer?"

"Are we making paper mâché turkeys for November? If so, can I make a plate of dressing and a sweet potato pie to go with mine?"

I took my seat beside my easel. "How creative! You don't feel that's excessive?"

"No, ma'am. A meal needs fixings."

"I'll take that under consideration." I offered him a smile and welcomed everyone to a new month of art and creativity.

"Don't cry, Callie. I didn't mean to get you in trouble. I'm sorry."

Suda Mae's half-whisper gained my attention. Instantly, I was on my feet, propelled in their direction. Hunkering down until eye-level, my heart lurched at the steady stream of tears rolling down my niece's face.

"Callandra, baby, what's wrong?"

Instantly, she flung herself against me, jarring my injured shoulder in the process. I gritted my teeth against a searing pain and held her as she sobbed.

"Come with me." Leading my niece to the rear of the room, I positioned her away from her classmates whose curious eyes were aimed in our direction. "What happened?"

"Uncle Willard paddled me for walking to school with Suda Mae and it hurts when I sit."

She twisted at her torso and lifted her skirt a bit, enough to display a bruise on the back of her thigh.

My blood ran cold. I was immediately nauseated.

Principal North had long ago banished paddling as discipline. Yet, Willard had dared to revisit the practice at my niece's expense?

It was payback for you and Gabe humiliating him.

An image of Willard sprawled on the ground in urine soaked pants wavered across my vision as I whirled toward the supply caddy and grabbed a pair of scissors.

"Everyone, sit quietly until I return."

I was out the door and down the hall headed toward Willard's classroom before better sense could get the best of me, fueled by fury. We hadn't encountered each other at the schoolhouse that day and I was too enraged to care if the meeting we were about to have proved fatal.

My rationale was impaired. I was livid that his spiteful cowardice had prompted him to harm my innocent beloved.

Snatching open the door to the fifth and sixth grade class, I entered the room, scissors tightly gripped, and simply stood there, staring.

"Miz Brinks...did you need something?"

The school secretary, Miss Evans, sat at Willard's desk, a science textbook in hand.

I glanced about the room as if expecting that monster to magically appear.

"If you're looking for Mr. Brinks, he had an appointment and left early. He didn't tell you?"

I slid the scissors behind my back without responding to her question. "My apologies for the interruption."

"Yes, ma'am, and I hope your shoulder feels better soon."

Acknowledging her well-wishes, I exited and leaned against the wall outside the door, thanking God He'd spared me from doing only He knew what. Clearing my mind as best as I could, I slowly headed back to my students, determined to see Oscar Richileu that afternoon. Appointment or no appointment, I needed Colemanville's one and only lawyer to begin divorce proceedings before some irreversible horror happened.

THE DISTANCE between Profit Coleman Elementary and Mr. Richelieu's wasn't extensive. That afternoon, in my urgency, it felt as if I couldn't cover the distance fast enough, that they were on two separate continents. I was prepared for a lengthy wait and the possibility of being denied his time without an appointment. Instead, I barely entered the anteroom before his secretary was ushering me into his inner sanctum as if my arrival was expected.

His manner was stoic yet conciliatory as if I was in need of comforting.

"I'm sorry things have taken a turn for you and Mr. Brinks, but thank you for coming in so quickly. My practice is to meet with both parties prior to drawing up papers. I found your husband's request rather unorthodox, but he was quite adamant about proceeding without you present due to... marital misconduct and alienation of affection."

I'd gone there to secure his services only to learn that Willard had been there earlier that day, initiating the legal resolution of our union.

"I intended no disrespect to you, Miz Brinks, but he was insistent. And quite vehement if not ill-tempered. I permitted him to sign the decree, but that doesn't make it binding. You are entitled to review it to determine if there's anything objectionable or that you wish changed."

Stunned yet ecstatic that Willard was of the same mind and chose to terminate our union, I read the simple two-page document like an automaton. I'd anticipated resistance and intentional objection once he learned of my desire to divorce him and could only thank God for this unanticipated turn of events. Mr. Richelieu's assistant was summoned to act as witness and notary. I signed with a flourish, utterly relieved.

Joy invaded my soul with the beauty and grace of a wilted flower lovingly resuscitated. My heart beat with wild excitement, its rush flooding my ears, nearly causing me to miss Mr. Richelieu's statement.

"Any division of property should prove relatively easy. Mr. Brinks isn't requesting anything beyond his share of joint assets, bank accounts included."

An odd sensation rushed through me that I dismissed. Material things felt trivial in the face of freedom.

I left understanding that the documents would be filed at the Onslow County courthouse and we'd be notified upon completion. Stepping into the brisk autumn day, I paused outside the office, hand to my chest, breathless with excitement that three years of a debilitating marriage could be ended in an instant.

Always know what you have and where you have it.

My soft-spoken grandmother believed in a wife's equal partnership and didn't espouse any "the little woman" ignorant notions. Particularly in fiscal affairs. Her cautionary advice flitting about me with the energy of hummingbird wings, I postponed heading to Greenie's in favor of the bank. I was disinterested in quibbling with Willard over dollars and cents, but knowing what we would be required to divide between us was necessary to my newfound self-sufficiency.

Lord, I'm ready to take care of myself. Please help me.

What I'd hidden in my box of sanitary needs couldn't sustain me indefinitely. I was unsure how long I could stay at Greenie's, but I refused to be a burden or wear out my welcome. I entered the Sheriff's office needing to know how much was at my disposal.

Colemanville's bank hadn't had its own separate facility since the flood of 1936. We'd endured a storm so severe

Copper Lake overflowed and threatened to become an ocean. When the floodwaters receded and downtown was inspected, the bank safe was found upside down in front of the Sheriff's office. Folks argued whether it had floated there on its own or was the consequence of a failed robbery attempt. Most said it didn't matter which. The safe had spoken. With the bank being damaged beyond repair, its new home would be the sheriff's office, a perfect detriment to would-be thieves and miscreants.

Sheriff Weaver sat reading the newspaper on his side of the premises when I entered. We exchanged brief pleasantries before I made my way to the one and only teller employed by Colemanville Bank & Trust, Mr. Saunders—part-time mortician, part-time banker.

"Afternoon, Miz Ilona." His expression wasn't unpleasant, just quizzical as he stared at me. "Did Mr. Willard forget something?"

"Pardon?"

"He wasn't here but...what would you say, Sheriff? Two or so hours ago?"

Sheriff Weaver answered without looking away from his newspaper. "Sounds about right."

An eerie sensation started at my feet, slowly rising through me. "What did he need?"

I asked the question despite the truth already spooling through me.

Willard had withdrawn our money. Our account was closed. Emptied.

Twenty-Three

"I wasn't aware of his...misbehaviors...particularly with that Pamela Sue...Pumpkin."

My sisters had wasted no time informing our mother of her soon to be former-son-in-law's misconduct. Unlocking the front door I'd never known to be locked to me, she allowed my entrance and dove into her sea of reasoning.

"It may have seemed that we sided with him on most things, but that isn't true, Ilona. We merely wanted peace...so you could be safe and provided for in our elderly age."

I struggled to keep my voice quiet, respectful as I entered my childhood home. "I'll provide for myself. I have art. I have a talent which my parents can't bring themselves to value or support."

Mother sniffed as if offended. "This world isn't friendly to regular Negro women. You certainly can't expect better treatment by doing or being something different."

I studied my mother, wondering why she didn't possess her own mother's quiet confidence and belief in women's abilities. Perhaps she had at some time in her existence only to exchange it along life's way for her own wellness and security.

Right then and there, I couldn't concern myself with our differences of opinion.

"Mother, where's Willard?"

"He wasn't feeling well and went to lay down."

"My luggage was placed on the porch, but he was allowed back into our home despite his mistreatment of me?"

Mother straightened her posture as if nobility. "This home belongs to your father and I. *We* decide who is or isn't welcome. Is that clear?"

My only response was turning away and heading down the hallway.

Mother trailed behind, lobbing questions that felt inane. "Is Willard telling the truth? Did you really and truly strike your husband?" She continued in my silence. "I didn't want to believe what your sisters said, but it's the only thing that would cause you to act so objectionably. You've fallen back into nonsense with Gabriel Thurman!"

Her words were ineffective pellets against my back as I flung my bedroom door open to an unseemly mess.

"Oh, dear Lord! What happened?" Mother stood beside me, shocked by the chaotic disarray that provided a greeting in a room that was typically pristine.

My clothing had been thrown about. Empty hangers decorated the bed. My dresser drawers were open, many of them emptied. Their contents covered the floor, several garments had been ripped, and the space at the bottom of the chifforobe where Willard's suitcase was normally housed now stood vacant. I took it all in, but none of it fully held my attention as did the box of feminine hygiene products laying on the dresser.

Carefully navigating the cluttered floor, I reached for the box only to find a handwritten note on top.

If you painted less niggardly subjects perhaps you'd have better success.

Ripping Willard's note to shreds, I let the pieces fall as they may, unaffected by his insult. I tried but failed to feel as unaffected by the fact that the box in which I'd squirreled away funds every payday now sat woefully empty.

"He took my money..."

Mother covered her mouth in bewilderment as she absorbed the aftermath of his mayhem. "He must have done all of this while Father and I were napping."

I sank onto the edge of the bed, expecting tears of outrage only to feel wild relief and a divine sense of freedom rise in my chest, brilliant as a mythical phoenix. Joy left me smiling, giddy.

He's gone. He stole my money from the bank and this box, but he couldn't take my happiness. I still have me. Gabe. My art in my shed...

An image of Willard destroying my artwork sent a fissure of fear from my feet to my belly. I bolted up and took off running.

"Ilona, what are you doing?"

My mother's voice was a distant echo as I raced through the house and down the back steps. The padlock that Willard cut and removed hadn't been replaced, leaving my artwork exposed to his vindictiveness. Running at full speed I could only pray that the work of my hands was safe.

Tossing the door open, I sagged in relief.

"They're here!" A quick inventory confirmed nothing was damaged or missing. Even my cherished box with its hummingbird painted on the lid was present. It was as if Willard had exhausted himself upending our room and lacked the requisite energy for additional violence and mayhem.

"Or maybe he wants to avoid another pants-pissing, rifle encounter with Gabe."

Sitting on the chair near my easel, I considered my sanctuary where order existed, unlike the bedroom I'd just fled.

The two spaces seemed indicative of my current state of affairs. The pending dissolution of marriage and the resurrection of a love I'd longed for and missed. The latter was sweet; the former tumultuous.

Willard had removed himself from my life and in the process taken money he had no right to. Not from our shared account or that box of hygiene products. Still, if accepting a financial loss proved the difference between marital bondage and liberty, he was welcome to keep every crookedly acquired penny.

"May it rot in his pockets and burn holes in his skivvies."

I laughed, only to remember I hadn't purchased my train ticket to Raleigh yet. Closing my eyes, I tried to recall what I had available in my coin purse. It wasn't much, and nowhere near enough to sustain me, let alone buy a train ticket in order to stand before the Nubian-Kush committee this weekend.

Cradling my hummingbird box against my breasts, I told myself I'd find a way. That was my prayer. And my promise.

THE BELL above the door chimed as I stepped into Iva's House of Beauty where Flo was applying her magic hands to her current customer, her great Aunt Sis, later that evening.

"Hey, Ilona! Good seeing you. Come on in, and welcome."

"Hey, Floretta."

"Well looka here! It's Madame Artiste herself. Paint anything pretty lately?"

I hugged Miss Sis and complimented the sheen of her pure white tresses before responding. "Actually...I have. It's not exactly a painting. More of a rendering." I removed the lipstick sketch I'd created at Greenie's from the portfolio I carried. "I know this probably sounds crazy..." I turned the paper for them to see. "But I may have drawn—"

"Mama Liberty?" Miss Sis lurched toward me, fixated on the drawing.

"I *knew* that was her that day I was visiting Mama at the cemetery!" Flo moved to her aunt's side, mouth open and wide-eyed.

"How'd you do this?" Hand on her chest, Miss Sis glanced at me briefly, preferring to favor the drawing with her attention.

I spared them the gory details of Willard and Pumpkin, settling instead on how Lady Liberty commandeered my drawing in a moment of personal crisis. "It was...surreal. I almost feel like it happened to someone else."

"Like you were possessed?"

I smiled at Flo's deduction. "Maybe. Yes."

"She has that effect." Aunt Sis uttered a sound of agreement. "Papa was sold away from her when he was just a boy, but he had a vivid memory of his mother and wanted his children to know and remember her through the stories he told." She chuckled gently while taking the drawing from me. "He wasn't nobody's artist by any stretch of the imagination, but one day he decided we needed to see her as well."

I listened, fascinated, as Miss Sis described the rough sketch her father presented to his offspring, the only visual likeness of a woman who bore the pain of eleven of her twelve children being sold away. Except for her father, Profit Coleman.

"I'm not sure where that drawing is today. Guess my sister Grace has it with all her other important things."

"In her Bible," Flo commented. "Is this why you stopped by? To share this drawing?"

"Yes...but also to ask something of you. Would you kindly consider allowing me to hold a ladies only art soiree here at the salon?"

The idea of hosting a soirée and selling my art hit me while seated in my art shed, making sense of all that had transpired. I was unclear about my future other than the fact that I had to get to Raleigh, but a quick accounting of what was in my coin purse proved enough for a one-way ticket to nowhere. Money might've been scarce, but my artwork wasn't. My hope was to sell enough to purchase train fare, but I dared to dream it would open a door to whatever my next steps in life might be.

Quickly, I extracted drawings from my portfolio and placed them on Flo's workstation.

"These're samples. Just enough for you to know what to anticipate."

"Ilona, you must be forgetting you already blessed me with a picture of Mama and that I asked you to paint my wedding portrait. I already know the caliber of your artistry and it's exquisite. So, yes. Now, when you wanna host this shindig?"

I bit my lip before softly answering, "Friday evening. After the DOLLs meeting."

"As in tomorrow's Wednesday...then the day after that?"

I laughed. "Yes, ma'am. And of course I'll pay you a commission from the total sales."

"You'll do no such thing."

"Yes I can and I will. Iva's House of Beauty is your livelihood the same as art is mine."

"Fine! If you pay to rent my place, then I'm paying you for the wedding portrait."

"Flo, you can't do that when that portrait is my gift to you."

"I'm a proud, Colored, business woman, Ilona. I can do whatever the heck I want to."

"Both of you need to hush up and just call it an even exchange. All this back and forth is hurting my ears."

We laughed at Miss Sis and shook hands on it.

A smile graced Flo's face as she propped her hands on her

hips and surveyed the salon she'd refurbished after inheriting it. "Well...with a few adjustments...I guess the space could be fitting for a quasi-art gallery. What do you think, Aunt Sis?"

Miss Sis returned the drawing to me, rather reluctantly. "I think I'm stepping in high cotton come Friday in Colemanville. Be sure to serve refreshments. Especially libations."

I SPENT that night and every night that week in Gabe's loving company after long days of diligently preparing for my art soirée. I curated pieces, created exhibition pamphlets and, with the help of Callie, Suda Mae, and Greenie, distributed invitations to women in the community. There was much to accomplish in three days, but it was accomplished with the help of my beloved. Including an additional family member.

My sister Olivia showed up Thursday evening at Iva's House of Beauty, ready to assist however needed. She was the middle child with Ravena and I cushioning her on one end and Viola and Theodora on the other. As the middle-born her personality and disposition had always been slightly more understanding than that of our eldest sisters. She was the peacemaker in between and I appreciated her presence.

"Livvie, Theodora and Viola made condemning comments about Ravena and I the other day. What did they mean?"

Olivia waved a dismissive hand. "Pay them no mind. They tend to be high strung from time to time."

I persisted as if she hadn't spoken. "They said I was as bad as Ravena and that we'd share a place in hell. That's not high strung. That's judgment and damnation."

Olivia paused her task of filling vases and bowls with water for the flowers that would lend their grace to tomorrow's event. She glanced about, making sure no one else was near enough to hear. "Do you know why Ravena moved to Philadelphia instead of coming home after graduating college?"

I'd visited my sister's home away from home on numerous occasions, especially during brief college holidays that I chose not to spend in Colemanville. Ravena and her housemate Nance were gracious hostesses and enthusiastic tour guides and I'd come to love the historical importance of the city and its bustling energy.

"Was it because she was blessed with a job at the newspaper?" It was high-paced and demanding. "But that's not enough to keep her from coming home to visit. So what is it?"

Olivia exhaled through pursed lips as if nervous. "Ravena avoids Colemanville because our parents disowned her because she and Nance...her housemate...aren't just friends." She continued in my blank-faced silence. "They're...*together*. Ravena likes women."

My shock was real, yet I held no condemnation toward my sister. How could I when sharing myself with a man who wasn't my husband defined me as an adulteress? Instead, my heart hurt for all the time she'd spent isolated and far from family because of our parents' rejection. I left Iva's House of Beauty that night knowing I too would likely incur their ostracism because of my choices. Yet, it was a chance I was willing to take. I'd married for their approval and would never again trade love for their acceptance.

GREENIE WAS A FARMER. She rose before the sun, in the dark of dawn. Still most mornings, after a night of laying in love with Gabe, I managed to make it back to her home before she awakened. The times I didn't she never batted a lash or offered recrimination. She simply smiled as if delighted by a delicious secret.

My nights with my love were enchanted. Divine. They

were stolen moments of laughter, loving, reclaiming and sharing lives we'd never imagined reconnecting. We even visited our precious Grotto Galleria. Whether there or the back storeroom of Gabe's family business, we recounted the days gone by, filling each other in on what we'd missed by not being in each other's presence. He sat as if enthralled by my less dramatic days in Colemanville. I listened, fascinated, to stories of his time as a soldier before being wounded, was humbled by his struggle to embrace life as a man whose life had changed physically.

"I went through it. The anger. Feeling sorry for myself. Not wanting to live. All kinds of mind trips." Even staying most nights at the family's business to spare his mother being witness to the night terrors and flashbacks to war that sometimes occurred, bringing him up from a deep sleep sweating and screaming. Readjusting proved more challenging than anticipated, but with God's grace he managed.

Initially, it took him longer to do even simple things after the loss of his arm, forcing him to slow down out of necessity. "Taught me to take my time and not be such a hot head."

He'd retrained himself to do with his left arm what he'd done with his right, shifting reliance onto that appendage until it became natural. Eating. Grooming. Woodworking and furniture building. Even writing. He demonstrated with the rubber, alternator fan belt straps he used to keep what remained of the right as healthy as the left, stretching those bands, building muscle through resistance. He was amenable to a prosthetic, but opposed to one reflecting white skin. I'd promised if ever he obtained one I'd paint it to match his beautiful complexion. His journey hadn't been easy, but life in an unfamiliar body matured him.

"I might come across hardened and grizzled some days, but I admit to knowing a kind of calm I didn't have before leaving a piece of me in Europe." He wanted to return to the continent as a civilian, particularly France. "Guess I wanna revisit the place that made me this version of myself."

"I love this version as much as I did the first."

"I survived the worst. And came home to the best." He kissed my forehead. "I'm grateful for you...for that."

Seated in his lap, facing him, I wrapped my legs about his waist and took my time branding him with kisses, sweet and warm enough to translate that I too shared such gratefulness.

Twenty-Four

"Honey, you're beautiful. Stop fidgeting."

"Greenie, I don't want to greet guests with my shoulder in this unappealing sling, looking like a pirate chicken."

"Chickens don't have arms. They have wings."

"You know what I mean."

"Listen to you two old fussing women." Dimple's laughter filled the storage space at the rear of Flo's salon. "How about we try this?"

Gingerly removing the sling provided by Doc Everett, she unwound the colorful silk scarf draped about her neck and created a fashionable substitute that complimented my dress. "How's that?"

The simple act of care left me teary-eyed, as did the support of my fellow DOLLs.

Dimple. Zayda. Greenie. Flo. Even Tippy. They'd foregone our Friday night DOLLs meeting in lieu of assisting me, ensuring all was in good order for tonight's soiree.

The week had been a whirlwind. Life had changed. I'd lost

family, finances, and a marriage. But I'd regained love, recovered freedom. I'd board a train to Raleigh tomorrow, different from the person I was when first applying to The Nubian-Kush Art Collaborative. This evolution of self hadn't been anticipated or straightforward, but I welcomed it. Wanted it. Would protect it with every ounce of my being. My divorce was pending, but I was Ilona Ann Robertson, a woman whose art spoke for her when others required my silence and acquiescence.

I was becoming.

"Folks are starting to arrive. And it's a lot of 'em!" Tippy poked her head around the corner, made her announcement, and disappeared.

"Well, you certainly chose the right hostess." Zayda's comment sparked laughter.

Mine was more nervous than pure.

Apparently, Nurse Zayda was in an intuiting mood. "I think we should have a word of prayer."

Instantly, our small gathering formed a circle and clasped hands. Zayda's prayer was sweet, brief yet inspiring, leaving me with a sense of peace.

"And may Ilona know that all is working for her good as it should. In the Lord's divine name we pray. Amen."

There were hugs and words of encouragement before the ladies departed. Only Greenie and I remained, hands clasped, smiling.

"Tonight is the beginning, LoLo. Your work will wow the world. Watch what I'm saying."

"You're not gonna get me crying, Clementine."

My dearest friend laughed. "You stay here and breathe until we announce your entrance."

She kissed my cheek and left, leaving me with God, myself, and my dreams.

When, moments later, I finally entered the salon, it was to

a vast gathering and applause that resonated in my soul like sweet thunder.

Overwhelmed, I took time to gather myself while looking at the ladies of Colemanville. They'd shown up in support of one of their own and their beauty outshone the exquisite transformation of Flo's salon.

Fragrant white camellias from Greenie's property floated in crystal bowls atop pedestals bearing my artwork. Gabe, Packer, and a group of their buddies had erected tall dividers from which hung billowy, pale blue curtains cordoning off the room and creating an intimate atmosphere as soft music played from a radio hidden from view. In the far corner on a beautifully appointed table, dainty sandwiches, slices of Dimple's melt-in-the-mouth pound cake, and a crystal punch bowl offered refreshment.

I offered opening words of welcome and appreciation, unable to take it all in. All were invited to view my work and, hopefully, purchase a desired piece. Even if they didn't, their presence and support meant the world to me.

"I am deeply touched that you're here. Please enjoy the evening. You'll find me in the center of the salon should you need me."

Each pedestal had been positioned intermittently to form a circle within the curtained perimeter. A raised platform with a chair and easel sat at its center. Amid applause, I took a seat on that makeshift dais and closed my eyes to ground myself before beginning a live sketch.

The women of Colemanville became a sweet smelling, living backdrop as I lost myself in my passion, sketching with a charcoal pencil, allowing a form to appear that was both near yet distant.

She stood in the center of a field of wildflowers, hair loose and curly as mine tended to be when freshly washed before a pressing comb touched it. Three bangles dangled on her wrist.

Her expression was broad yet serene, as if life had been both taxing and triumphant.

"It's a self-portrait."

The whispered words invaded my concentration. Glancing back, I found Olivia. And my mother. They stood arm-in-arm, faces awed.

My quick glance about the room resulted in no sighting of Theodora or Viola. A miniscule ping of disappointment shot through me only to dissipate as quickly as it came. I was in my element, allowing no place for regret. Returning my attention to my mother and sister, I smiled, truly blessed by their supportive presence and the encouraging telegram Ravena sent that day, now tucked safely in my pocket.

"She's you, Ilona Ann." Mother pointed to the rough, unfinished sketch, unadorned by paint or pigment. "She's beautiful...and you're brilliant."

I returned her soft smile that held admiration and repentance before reexamining the exquisite creature on my canvas.

She was me, yet different, a semblance of me from my past or my future. Which, I wasn't certain. Gazing at the women engaged by and discussing my art as they huddled about it, I simply embraced the watercolor sweetness of the present.

I STOOD before The Nubian-Kush Collaborative the next day without a sling from Dimple or Doc Everett, refusing to negatively impact my chances by being viewed as incapacitated or an invalid. Instead, I clenched my teeth through pain and completed my presentation buoyed by the support of the women of Colemanville.

Lord, thank You for blessing me to sell so many paintings! It was amazing.

Not only had I earned enough proceeds to purchase my train ticket, but what remained exceeded my weekly pay from

Profit Coleman Elementary and would be used to open *my own* bank account first thing Monday morning. Add to that the fact that I received two commissioned orders. I was ecstatic.

"Thank you, Mrs. Brinks, for your in-depth and engaging interview. Please have a seat in the waiting area to allow the committee to make a final assessment now that we've met both you and the other candidate."

"Yes, ma'am." I turned to exit only to pause a moment. "If you would, please note it's Miss Robertson not Mrs. Brinks."

I was still legally a wife, yet I was already liberated in my mind.

Sitting in the waiting room with the other candidate was both torturous and pleasant. It was refreshing discussing the craft with a fellow artisan, a young Negro man from Kentucky. But on the reverse side, he was my competition, the final hurdle between being named senior artist.

Twenty minutes felt like twenty years. By the time the committee chairperson approached the waiting room, my shoulder throbbed and my foot restlessly bobbed.

"Thank you both for your patience. We'd like to share our final decision with you in alphabetical order by last name. Mr. Ashby, follow me please."

He had the decency to wish me good luck before departing.

Lord, since I was a little girl drawing pictures and hosting art shows for my dolls, all I've ever wanted to do is celebrate the glory of Your creation in art form. Let Your will be done in all things...but I'd really love to win this fellowship.

The "amen" to my silent prayer had barely crossed my lips before the door of the inner chamber opened and my competitor burst into the waiting area, his face shining with ecstasy.

"They chose me! I got the..."

He fell silent, realizing his joy was being expressed to his competition.

Swallowing abject disappointment, I stood and offered a congratulatory handshake.

"Miss Robertson, do you mind giving us a moment of your time before leaving?"

I wished The Nubian-Kush Collaborative's newest fellow well before doing as requested. I sat before the committee, telling myself that all things were as they should be.

I stepped out of fear and into courage simply by applying. I value myself for trying.

Repeatedly reciting my mantra to lessen the sadness claiming the edges of my disposition, I nearly missed what the committee chairperson was saying.

"...it's a new program in its infancy, but we'd be delighted if you'd consider representing the Collaborative."

"My apologies, but could you please repeat that?"

There was good-natured laughter that tapered off as the committee chairperson restated what I'd heard, but had difficulty receiving.

"As a pilot program focused on art around the world, *L'Art du Monde* is committed to equality. That's why they reached out to us hoping we might recommend a Negro delegate for its inaugural launch. Please don't see it as tokenism. You are guaranteed the same award package and will be treated with the same dignity as the other artists in residence from various countries around the globe."

"I served in the military during the war and can attest that, by and large, the French are quite different," another committee member added.

The program benefits were similar to that of the Nubian-Kush award. Lodging. A monthly stipend. Opportunities for personal and artistic development and advancement. The blissfulness of solely focusing on one's art in order to produce a vast body of work. Camaraderie with fellow artists in residence. A gallery exhibition.

The major difference?

The yearlong *L'Art du Monde* program was in Paris, France.

"You'd be required to provide us with quarterly reports on your progress and experience. And we would like to host a symposium upon your return and program completion. We understand this is a lot to consider. How much time would you need before providing an answer, Miss Robertson?"

"None." I exhaled the breath I'd unconsciously been holding. "I'd be honored to serve as delegate of The Nubian-Kush Collaborative for *L'Art du Monde* in Paris, France."

Twenty-Five

"Call me on Sundays. I want a postcard every month. And bring back some fancy French perfume that'll help me seduce some poor, unsuspecting farmer."

Greenie's sniffled instructions reverberated against my cheek as we clung together, laughing through our tears.

"Promise. I will."

"I'm so proud of you, LoLo."

"I know. And I'm proud of you."

"Proud of me?" She pulled back and stared. "For what?"

"For having the courage to keep living in Conroy's absence."

"Yeah...well...bring me that perfume and maybe I can trap a new man sweet as him."

I laughed and kissed her cheek, thankful for love. Thankful for Greenie. Our DOLLs. My family. And Colemanville's community that had gathered at the depot despite December's intermittent rain to wish me farewell with all the pomp and circumstance due someone famous. In the eight weeks since the art soirée, I'd continued to sell existing pieces and acquire new commissions. I'd finished the painting of she who was me but not me—the precious one dressed in white in a field of colorful wildflowers—and painted Flo's wedding portrait. Conversely, I'd intentionally left the lipstick drawing of Lady Liberty in its raw state, preferring its simple majesty to perfection. Framing it, I'd gifted it to Miss Sis and in exchange received her teary appreciation.

Loving life and all its imperfections, I hugged Greenie once again before embracing my DOLLs and sharing farewells with my parents.

"We never meant to stifle you. We simply didn't think this world could make space for a Colored woman with your gifts and talents." Mother cradled my face and kissed my forehead. "Thank God for showing us our ignorance."

I wiped a tear from her cheek before bending to kiss my father seated in his wheelchair. He smiled and patted my cheek as Theodora took my elbow to navigate me away from the gathering.

"Come on, now. The train's about to leave. Put these in your pocketbook."

I looked down at the satin pouch she placed in my lace glove-covered hand. "What is it?"

"Peppermints. And ginger drops," Viola advised, marching along on the opposite side. "You've never been on an ocean liner and it's a long crossing. Plus, the winter might make for rough waters."

Olivia, who was steps ahead, glanced back and added, "They'll help with any seasickness you might experience."

Accepting the candies and their care, I boarded the train where my luggage was already stowed and stood in the entryway, waving and blowing kisses as the train began to roll.

"Have fun, Auntie Ilona, but don't forget to come home!"

I placed a hand over my heart, moved by their sweetness as Callie and Suda Mae skipped along the depot platform, tossing flower petals as if flower girls for the railway until the platform ended and all they could do was wave.

I rushed to my seat and lowered the window, fluttering my handkerchief until Colemanville was a mirage in the distance. Only then did I sit and wipe away tears of joy not pain.

I am on my way to France!

I took a moment to gather myself, feeling blissfully overwhelmed. Thanksgiving. Christmas. I'd had two months, two glorious Colemanville holidays to adjust to the notion. Still, it felt surreal that a little country, Colored girl from a small all-Black town was headed to the art capital of the world. Now, the New Year was two days away, waiting with all of its glory and greatness.

I am going to France. It will leave its mark on me. I will leave my mark on it as well…no matter how small.

My heart was full of sunshine despite the cold rain outside as I opened my pocketbook to retrieve the small picture card from Gabe. It was double-sided. Laminated. One side bore a beautiful hummingbird flitting above a flower; the other heralded the tiny bird's significance.

Independence. Fierce fighter. Intelligence. Good news. Resilience.

You're all these things and more to me, Sweet Rivers.

We'd been discreet, allowing my divorce to be finalized before walking in the openness of our love and affection. That didn't mean we'd gone without suspicion. Particularly from Miz Thurman.

I took care to eradicate traces of my presence and time with Gabe from the furniture storeroom whenever we were together. I even insisted he resume time at home versus sleeping at the store regularly. That didn't keep his mother from raising an eyebrow and smiling like she knew something whenever she saw me. It made me blush and was embarrassing. But nothing and no one could deter me from loving Gabriel

Thurman or being loved by him. Not failure in marriage. And definitely not Pumpkin.

She'd spread whispers that Gabe had fathered her child. Folks did the math real quick, determining he'd been in Europe fighting a war when her child was conceived. Besides, as noted before, Pumpkin's daughter looked so much like him she could've been Councilman Ashwood's twin.

I wasn't sure what she hoped to gain by lying, but it must've irked her not getting it. Two weeks before Christmas, Pamela Sue "Pumpkin" Minkins packed herself and her daughter up and left town with a traveling salesman. She'd had enough of living in a "one-cow town" and chose to head to higher ground and big city lights with all of its "choreographering."

I forgot about Pumpkin and laughed to keep from crying.

What kind of lunacy made me tell him not to come today?

Gabe and I had shared our private goodbye last night, slowly loving each other in ways meant to store memories deep in our bones. Our flesh. I made him promise not to come to the depot to see me off. He'd objected so soundly, we'd disagreed so strongly, it threatened to tarnish the sweetness of our loving.

"What kind of damn sense does that make, me not being there to see you off when I won't see you for a whole year, Sweet Rivers? Especially, seeing as how we ain't been too long reunited."

"That's precisely why I'm asking you *not* to be there, Gabe?" I'd broken down into tears. "I don't want to see your beautiful face and give myself a reason not to get on that train."

I'd given up and married Willard after losing a once-in-a-lifetime kind of a love. Now that he was mine again, I was afraid that *being afraid* of losing us might lead me to forfeit this God given opportunity and that I'd wind up not leaving Colemanville.

He'd stomped out into the cold December night and stayed so long I'd wrapped myself in the quilt, ready to go in search of him only for him to reenter the storeroom, wet-eyed but cooperative.

"You get on that train to New York tomorrow. Sail to France. Knock that art world on its ass...then marry me when you get back."

It was a whispered proposal I wholeheartedly accepted, one that led to the sweetest love-making I'd ever experienced.

"I love you, Gabriel Thurman." Kissing the hummingbird card I held, I pressed my head against the window and cried until exhaustion-driven sleep was merciful and came for me.

"Excuse me, miss. Is this seat taken?"

I startled slightly at the sound of a deep, masculine voice rolling through my sleep.

Quickly, I sat up, the rocking of the train reminding me where I was, and straightened my skirt about my knees. "No, sir, it's—"

Staring at the tall gentleman awaiting a response, I felt as if I was hallucinating. *"Gabe?"*

He tipped the brim of his fedora and bowed his head. "At your service, *mademoiselle*."

I sprang from my seat, needing to touch him to prove he wasn't an illusion before hurling myself into his embrace when finding he was real. *"What're you doing here?"*

"Escorting the prettiest lady I've ever laid eyes on to the Big Apple."

Speech abandoned me and I dropped onto my seat.

"That is...with your permission." He removed the hat from his head, stood there suited in his Sunday's best, handsome and erect. "I don't wanna undermine your independence or interfere with your experience, baby. It's just...a whole year...and an ocean of distance..."

I patted the seat and waited for him to sit. "When did you plan this?"

"What makes you think it ain't spontaneous?"

"Because I know you, Gabe Thurman."

He chuckled quietly. "The week after Thanksgiving. It was supposed to be my surprise to you, but then you went and pulled the rug out from under my feet telling me not to show my ugly face at the station this morning."

I laughed and stroked his strong chin, loving his sensitivity and kindness. His generosity. The custom frames he built for my customers and their canvases. The drying rack he fashioned for my students to hang their work in art class. His constant care and protective nature. The way he saw and valued Ilona Ann. But most of all, I cherished the ways he shared himself with me, his love, and absolute acceptance.

"I've never called you ugly and if I did I'd be lying. You're the handsomest escort a woman could want."

"Yeah, well, I had Packer haul me to the Greenville station to catch up with you. We barely did, but thank God we made it."

I kissed him. "Come with me to Europe."

He leaned away as if I had two heads. "Woman, what's wrong with you? First, you don't want me anywhere near the train station. Now, you wanna drag my ass to France?"

I swatted his thigh and laughed softly. "Not now. When my *L'Art du Monde* program is finished, meet me in Paris."

"Why?"

"You said you wanted to visit France again. And I want to get married in the city of lights."

A slow grin spread across his face. He kissed me softly. "Sweet Rivers, you ain't gotta ask me twice."

Generations: The Series

Book 1: *Forever Beautiful*
Book 2: *Wandering Beauty*
Book 3: *Watercolor Whispers*
Book 4: *Graceful Watercolors*
Book 5: Coming February 2025
Book 6: Coming February 2025
Book 7: Coming May 2025
Book 8: Coming May 2025
Book 9: Coming August 2025
Book 10: Coming August 2025

Book 4

Enjoyed Book 3? Don't stop there! Meet Ilona's beautiful descendant, Ella Caswell.

Graceful Watercolors
by Suzette Riddick

After graduating college, Ella Caswell left her hometown of Colemanville, North Carolina, determined to pursue her dream of becoming a renowned painter and photographer. With her heart set on capturing the beauty of the world through her art, she traveled far and wide, perfecting her craft.

Ella's once adventurous, nomadic lifestyle became a necessity when she found herself on the run to protect her son, Manny. Exhausted both mentally and physically, she was determined to keep moving, always staying one step ahead. As the weight of her situation grew heavier, Ella longed for stability and a place where Manny could feel safe and secure. Returning to her hometown of Colemanville, she hoped to find the peace she so desperately needed. But the past had a way of catching up, and Ella soon realized that some battles must be faced head on.

Amid the turmoil, Ella was determined to create a loving

home for her son, rekindle a long-forgotten dream, and open her heart to the possibility of love. Will her past extinguish her future, or will grace find a way? Discover the answer in Graceful Watercolors.

Other Books by This Author

HISTORICAL FICTION

Forever Beautiful

My Name is Ona Judge

The Dust Bowl Orphans

The Girl at the Back of the Bus

The Art of Love

Taffy

CONTEMPORARY FICTION

This Time Always

Basketball & Ballet

The Birthday Bid

My Joy

When Perfect Ain't Possible

Living on the Edge of Respectability

CHILDREN'S FICTION

My Tired Telephone

Wonderful Readers

You're the backbone of the literary community. Without your support, writers' works would collect dust and go unnoticed. So, I thank you for noticing me.

If you enjoyed *Watercolor Whispers* I'd be honored if you'd share that enjoyment by posting a review on Amazon.com and/or other platforms such as Goodreads or BookBub. If you're using a Kindle, the app lets you post a review when finishing the book. How cool and convenient is that? So, *please* take a minute to share your perspective. Your review can be as brief as a sentence, but it has tremendous impact. And by all means, tell a friend!

Let's Connect

One of my favorite aspects of being an author is connecting with my readers and discussing literary things. Here are some of the ways you can connect with me. If you're part of a book club/reading group and are interested in a virtual visit, check out the Book Club Love section on my website!

Facebook: Suzette D. Harrison Books
Goodreads: Suzette D. Harrison
Instagram: suzettedharrison
LinkedIn: Suzette Harrison
Newsletter Sign-up: www.sdhbooks.com
Pinterest: Suzette D. Harrison Books
Website: www.sdhbooks.com
YouTube: Suzette Harrison

Acknowledgments

Thank You, Lord God my Creator and Source, for allowing me yet another opportunity to share the gifts You've given me. I am forever grateful for Your countless blessings.

Thank you my beloved sister, friend, collaborator of the Generations Series, Suzette Riddick—my Twinny Twin. God and the ancestors must have whispered in our mothers' ears and told them to give us a shared name so we'd find each other. It took some time, but we locked arms and brought this series to life! Our mothers are pleased and satisfied.

Thank you to my husband and children who graciously allow me to be me and write to my heart's content. Without your love I couldn't do this.

Blessings to my extended family (mother, sisters, brother, nephews, and nieces), and my circle of beloveds. I truly value you.

Grace and peace to every reader, book club, my street team, and book promoter who lovingly and graciously support me. I appreciate you immensely.

About the Author

Award-winning author Suzette D. Harrison grew up in a home where reading was required, not requested. Her literary "career" began in junior high school with the publishing of her poetry. She pays homage to Alex Haley, Gloria Naylor, Alice Walker, Langston Hughes, and Toni Morrison as legends who inspired her creativity. However, it was Maya Angelou's *I Know Why the Caged Bird Sings* that unleashed her writing. The bestselling author is a wife and mother of two and holds a culinary degree in Pastry & Baking. Suzette is currently cooking up her next novel...in between batches of cookies.